REESE, John Henry

Texas gold [by] John Reese.   Garden City,
N.Y., Doubleday [c]1975.
186p.   (A Double D Western)

TEXAS GOLD

Books by John Reese

SURE SHOT SHAPIRO
THE LOOTERS
SUNBLIND RANGE
PITY US ALL
SINGALEE
HORSES, HONOR AND WOMEN
JESUS ON HORSEBACK: THE MOONEY COUNTY SAGA
ANGEL RANGE
THE BLOWHOLERS
THE LAND BARON
THE BIG HITCH
SPRINGFIELD .45-70
WEAPON HEAVY
THEY DON'T SHOOT COWARDS
THE SHARPSHOOTER

TEXAS GOLD

JOHN REESE

DOUBLEDAY & COMPANY, INC.
GARDEN CITY, NEW YORK
1975

All of the characters in this book are purely fictional, and any resemblance to actual persons, living or dead, is coincidental.

Library of Congress Cataloging in Publication Data

Reese, John Henry.
  Texas gold.

  I. Title.
PZ3.R25673Te [PS3568.E43]   813'.5'4
ISBN 0-385-08550-8
Library of Congress Catalog Card Number 74-12705

For Tom and Pat Reese

CHAPTER ONE

Hewitt let his cards pile up untouched. The man at his right, Dory Ketchum, the county clerk, took his up as they were dealt, separated them into suits, and then could not wait to bid. "Open," he said, as the last cards came out, three at a time. "Bid 'em high and sleep in the street."

Hewitt fanned his cards, using only his left hand. He saw a run in diamonds, both spade aces, and the king and queen of clubs. "Two-sixty," he said. He dropped the hand on the table, face down, and took out a cigar.

The dealer picked up his cards. "Boys, you mean to make it expensive for me, don't you?" he murmured. Watching him, Hewitt saw a look of amazement start across the soft, middle-aged face. It went out like a light, and the face became blank as the man got it under control.

Hewitt struck a match and applied it to his cigar. "Up to you, sir," he said.

The dealer looked at the three-card kitty, before meeting Hewitt's eyes. "Very expensive," he said, in his soft voice. "Very *damn* expensive! Two sixty-five."

"Two seventy-five," said Dory.

"Two-eighty," said Hewitt.

Again the dealer glanced at the kitty, and then at Hewitt. A dozen or so men watched the game, in the hot little office of the county clerk. There were windows open on two sides, but the humid breeze off the Gulf offered little relief, when it blew at all. In summer, in the coastal plains of East

Texas, men watched a pinochle game with the same rapt attention they would have given to a funnel-shaped cloud on the horizon. Anything that broke the monotony of heat and humidity was important, whether welcome or not.

"And five," said the dealer.

"Two-ninety," Dory said promptly.

"It's bedtime for small boys. This is a man's game from now on," said Hewitt. "Three-ten."

"Pass."

Dory brooded passionately over his cards for a moment, forehead in hand. "Oh hell, pass!" he said.

"Turn them over," said Hewitt.

There was a queen of spades in the kitty, plus two junk hearts. Hewitt bunched the kitty into his hand, discarded all but one heart, and said, "Gentlemen, let's play diamonds." He showed his meld—150 trump, 40 pinochle, 20 clubs.

They were playing what was called "tournament rules" here in the East Texas dunes: Four hands made a game. Aces and tens counted ten each, kings and queens, five each. Open at 200 in three-handed, 150 in four-handed. It made a good, fast evening of pinochle, many games instead of one long one, and low man bought the beer.

Hewitt led his trump ace, came back with his trump queen, and punched the other ace out of the dealer. "Thanks, Doc," he said. "I feel better."

He did not look up to see the reaction to the nickname, but he knew he had brought one out, just as surely as he had the other ace of trump. They played the cards rapidly. Hewitt was run out of trump before he could shoot for the last trick, but he made his bid exactly. Dory picked up the cards and began shuffling them.

"Real fine state of affairs, he told me, yes sir, he did. Real fine state of affairs it is when Texas hospitality is repaid this way. So my daddy told me," he drawled.

"Beware of slick-talking strangers," said Hewitt.

"Yes, sir! You hold all the aces but you still buy the beer."

The dealer of the previous hand said nothing. The cards had been dealt out for this last hand of the game, when the station agent from the railroad came shuffling into the room, and pushed his way through the watchers to Hewitt's side. "Telegram for you, Mr. Hewitt," he said. "I brung it right over, like you said."

"Thank you, sir," said Hewitt. He took the telegram but did not open it, because there were too many eyes behind him. He handed the agent two one-dollar bills, gave him a grateful, man-to-man smile, and picked up his cards. The agent went out importantly.

"Open," Hewitt said. He looked at the man with the soft, middle-aged face. "Up to you, Doc."

Doc may have looked a little annoyed. "Two-fifty," he said, after a glance at his cards.

"Pass," said Dory.

"Pass," said Hewitt.

Doc almost smiled, but not quite. He called trumps, melded 120, and made it in a swiftly played hand. Dory added up the score: Hewitt 595, Doc 510, and Dory 235.

"I guess I've had enough," Doc said. "Too hot. A man can't think."

"I play pinochle so I don't have to think," said Hewitt, "but I've had enough, too."

"Come on, I'll buy the goddamn beer, and then I've got to get some work done," said Dory. "Fine state of affairs, Daddy used to tell me, when a man has to buy the beer in his own game."

"Dory, I'm going to have to pass the beer today," said Hewitt. "I've got too many things to do."

The soft-faced man apologized too, saying he rarely drank anything alcoholic. The county clerk went out, taking the loafers with him. Left at the desk in the back room of his office were Hewitt and the man he had called Doc. Hewitt held the telegram without opening it, and looked over it at the other.

"Why?" he said. "Why did you do it, in a pinochle game for fun?"

The man's rather shapeless face suddenly was downright attractive, with a wide smile. "Oh," he said, "it gets dull. Anything to break the dullness."

"First time in Texas?"

"Yes, why?"

"They take such things seriously here. I don't think I would want that deck lying around."

"You caught me at it real quick, didn't you?"

"Not until the next-to-the-last game."

"Well, you sure screwed me up good then!"

It had been no problem for Hewitt to figure out who was thumbnailing the aces and face cards, once he realized it was being done. Dory was not even a very good pinochle player, and he lacked the soft hands—especially fingertips —with which to read nailmarks. There was nothing at stake in the game that Hewitt could see. He played a few hands, to make sure, before thumbnailing the nines and jacks, too. He made sure his marks were deeper, easier to read, than Doc's. And now he still did not know why Doc had done it.

He opened his telegram, which was from his partner, Conrad Meuse, in Cheyenne. It said:

BIG Q STOPPED HERE SAID ONLY PASSING THROUGH
STOP DO NOT BELIEVE HIM STOP GAVE HIM

AUSTIN ADDRESS STOP ADVISE SOONEST IF RETURN DELAYED.

The man across the table was methodically and a little dreamily tearing up the deck and throwing it into the old nail keg that served Dory Ketchum as a wastebasket. "Ever run into anybody by the name of Morton Kiely?" he said suddenly.

"I'm not sure. The name is familiar, somehow, but I don't place him," Hewitt said.

"Then how come you to call me 'Doc?'"

The man threw the last of the torn cards away, and closed his hands together under his chin, his elbows on the table. Hewitt pulled his mind back from the telegram, and decided to go along with this fool, to see what was on his mind, mostly because the man was not such a fool as he seemed to want to look.

"Your name is Doc Nolan," he said, "and you used to have a little troupe of actors. Give me a minute, and I'll tell you the name."

"Darien and Truro's Classics."

"You got into trouble—homicide, wasn't it?—in Toledo—"

"Cleveland. That's all cleared up. I can go anywhere in the country, and nobody wants me."

Hewitt said impatiently, "I believe you. I'm not interested in you."

"And your name is Bing. Let's see, Robert Bing."

"Richard," said Hewitt. "What's the point of all this?"

"I just wonder what you're doing here."

"Getting ready to go home. I might wonder about you, too, except that it's none of my business."

Doc Nolan said, "A detective by the name of Richard Bing. I was with Mort Kiely when he died. He had no regrets about going, crippled up the way he was. He knowed he was dying, and he spent a lot of them last couple of days, going back over the way he'd spent his life."

"Misspent it," Hewitt said.

"I reckon Mort would be the first to endorse that," Doc Nolan said with a smile. "A few things, though, was worth living for, he said. A nun who used to teach him his lessons, when he was a kid. A horse he owned in Kansas. And a detective by the name of Richard Bing, hired to prove a case of murder on him."

"To find a murderer," Hewitt said. "I never agree to prove anything on anybody. Kiely didn't do the killing. I found the man who did and got paid for it. Kiely didn't owe me anything."

"Only your name was Richard Bing," Nolan insisted.

"What's the difference? In my business, you use many names that aren't your own."

"The difference is, Mr. Hewitt, it proves I'm not such a fool as I look. I knowed who you was. I never seen you before, did I? Yet from what Mort Kiely told me on his deathbed, I picked you out. So I ain't such a fool, am I?"

"You are if you're going to go around Texas, thumbnailing cards and carrying a knife," said Hewitt. "You can get lynched for packing a knife if you go very far west of here. It's not considered a fair weapon in Texas."

Nolan moved limply and apparently without speed, but his right hand had dipped into the sleeve of his left arm, and he had the knife in his hand and was half on his feet, leaning forward across the table. Hewitt moved at the same time, jumping up and flinching back from the knife. He yanked the handkerchief out of the breast pocket of his coat, and wiped his forehead with it.

"You've had your joke, now put it away," he said.

Nolan smiled. Hewitt stuffed the handkerchief back into his pocket, and flipped the shot-filled, leather sap out of the same pocket. He swung it in a short arc, and hit Nolan's hand smartly. The knife clattered to the table. Hewitt picked it up and dropped it on the table closer to him.

"Don't ever pull a weapon on me, Mr. Nolan," he said. "I have no sense of humor about it."

Nolan nodded. "Give me back my knife."

Hewitt flipped it across the table with his fingertips. "Better pack that away in your valise until you leave Texas. Nobody else thinks it's funny here, either."

Nolan unbuttoned his shirt, to slide the knife into the sheath he wore next to his body. "Habit," he said, "but I agree, it's one I should break, for my health. And it wasn't a joke, Mr. Hewitt, or Mr. Bing, as the case may be."

"Hewitt."

"You're a detective. Want to make some money?"

"No."

"A lot of money. Just one *hell* of a lot."

"It would have to be a lot. We're probably the most expensive agency in the country."

Nolan took some coins from his pocket. He clinked them together inside his closed fist. "The idee," he said, with a crooked grin, "is to mystify you a little. Catch your interest! Now you see it, now you don't. Gentleman in the new blue shirt, would you keer to guess which walnut shell conceals the pea? One free guess, ladies and gentlemen. Now watch carefully—"

He gave Hewitt a glimpse of bright gold, but when he opened both hands, the coins had disappeared. He leaned across the table, snapped the fingers of his right hand, and produced the three fifty-dollar gold pieces from the end of Hewitt's nose. He let them slide out of his palm to the table with a little graceful flourish.

"Now you see it, now you don't. Hundred and fifty dollars, newly minted. Aren't they beauties, Mr. Hewitt?"

Hewitt did not touch the coins. "Yes," he said, "but they're not gold. Why all the hocus-pocus, Mr. Nolan?"

"They're all I've got now, everything in the world," said Nolan. "I want to sell them to you, and tell you where you can probably find fifty thousand dollars' worth of them. That's only the first run. There'll be a million, before they quit. Ort to be a right smart reward for that, wouldn't you think?"

"The government isn't much for paying rewards. When I work for them, it's to make friends. Where did you get those beauties?"

"Oh no! First, let's make a deal."

Hewitt shook his head. "No deal. Have you passed any of those coins, Mr. Nolan?"

"No, do you think I'm a fool?"

"We all are, on occasion."

"I haven't passed any. I took these as my salary for two weeks of work. A man's inclined to get lit up when he finishes a job, and to me, that's one of the sacred rights of the lowly working man. I got good and boiled, Mr. Hewitt, or I never would have taken slick money," said Nolan.

"You'll want to know, I bet, if the feller that passed it on me is in the business of passing slicks. No, he ain't. That's my judgment, anyhow. Well then, you'll ask, where did he get them? I'm pretty sure I could tell you that. I think there's close to a thousand more of them bright beauties where these came from. I don't know what he paid for them, but he's stuck for a lot of good, hard cash. Now, if you was to offer to get that good money back for him, and at the same time, turned this slicker that's making them in to the United States Treasury—"

Hewitt picked up the coins and examined them. The engraving was good enough to pass a hurried inspection, meaning that they had been stamped out by good steel dies made by a master craftsman. The milling around the edges seemed to him to have been die-stamped too, with the coin flat at the time. The bottom surface would have been rough around the edges, with this technique—and sure enough, there were signs of a high-speed, wire-brush burnisher where the milling shreds had been eliminated.

The coins were obviously of brass, to judge by the way they rang on the table, but they *looked* like gold, and they lacked the slick feeling that made counterfeit gold coins so easily detected. These "slicks" had been coated with a thin wash of gold, meaning that the maker had had access not only to excellent diemaking and stamping talent, but a chemical plating shop, too.

"Pretty good, aren't they?" said Nolan.

"Yes. Whoever made them has an investment in them, and it's a big enough investment to make you wonder if he's going to try to pass them a few at a time," said Hewitt.

"That's what I said, ain't it?"

"How much do you want for these, Mr. Nolan?"

"Sell them to you for half of what they cost me. Seventy-five bucks, Mr. Hewitt."

"Nothing doing. I'll give you two hundred," said Hewitt, "and you'll sign a receipt for it. I mean to be able to prove at any time that I didn't buy them to pass them at a profit. Now, where did you get them?"

Nolan dropped his voice. "From a fella by the name of Tommie Taylor, and I think he stole them from his dad. The one-six-one ranch, up southeast of San Antonio."

"What were you doing that was worth seventy-five dollars a week to Tommie Taylor?"

"Trying to teach him a few card tips. Mr. Hewitt, there's nobody on earth more worthless than a rich man's kid who won't grow up. I knowed these was slicks, minute I laid eyes on them, but I was so glad to get shet of that man, I'd've took Chinese money."

He told Hewitt how to find the 161 ranch. Hewitt took him to the bank, where Alf Hughes, the president, hurried to serve him personally. It had taken Hewitt just eight days to break a forgery case that could have cost the bank $21,000, and he had recovered most of the money, too.

"Met with my board this morning, Mr. Hewitt, and they feel the same as me. You work too cheap. We'll pay you another thousand dollars, sir, if you'll accept it," said Hughes.

Hewitt shook his head. He had as much greed as any man, but it was still not great enough to cloud his judgment. The bank's payment for two weeks' work, at $500 per week, plus expenses of $688.81, had already been forwarded to Conrad Meuse in Cheyenne.

"I would rather have your good will, and know you'll be telling people that we give value received, than another thousand dollars," said Hewitt.

"Now you know you have our good will. You know that!"

"I find I'm going to be around here a few days yet, and I'm short of cash. I'm wiring my partner to send you five hundred, to my account, but meanwhile I want to write my friend a check for two hundred, and I'd like to borrow a sheet of good paper and a stub pen."

"Sir, anything this bank can provide is yours."

Hewitt dictated the receipt, and had Doc Nolan write it in his own hand:

Received of Jefferson Hewitt, the sum of two hundred dollars ($200.00) in payment for three (3) coins with a face value of fifty dollars ($50.00) each, be-

lieved to be false and counterfeit, and surrendered as evidence.

Eoain B. Nolan

Yes, Hewitt thought, watching Nolan affix his big, elaborate signature, but evidence of what . . . ? He handed over the two hundred dollars cheerfully, and parted friends with Doc Nolan, cardsharp, actors' manager, prestidigitator of no mean ability, knife fighter, and the Lord knew what else. Hewitt liked characters like Nolan. They were shifty but not thieves, smart without having good sense, cynical without being poisonously bitter about it. Some of Hewitt's best friends, of which he had only a few, were from that lapland where honesty lapped over into dishonesty to no one's real hurt.

There was no hotel here, but there was a good rooming and boarding house much used by railroaders and salesmen. He had planned on leaving on the evening train, but now he hurried back to Mrs. Latimore and arranged to stay a few more days. He spent a good hour composing three telegrams in his room. The first, to his partner, employed a word, "clue," that Hewitt detested. Conrad loved clues. You could get more out of Conrad on a clue than you could on a first mortgage. This wire said:

DELAYED AUSTIN STOP HAVE CLUE BIG NEW CASE STOP SEND FIVE HUNDRED CARE CLIENT BANK STOP WATCH Q HE IS SLY.

The next wire went to Denny McGucken, whom Hewitt had known years ago as a Chicago policeman. Denny had read law and passed the bar. He was now some kind of attorney for the Treasury in Washington. Hewitt had not seen him for years, but he was happy that he had thrown most of the credit and all of the publicity for that old

Chicago case to Denny. He had thought that maybe Denny would come in handy someday, being a man of both wit and ambition; and today he had. To Denny, he said:

HAVE THREE SLICK FIVE OH PIECES STOP BELIEVE BUSHELS DUE STOP GLAD ASSIST AS PATRIOTIC DUTY BUT CAN USE HELP STOP PLEASE FORWARD ALL YOU KNOW CONDON HOUSE AUSTIN NO LATER TWO WEEKS WARMEST REGARDS.

And to Johnny Quillen, chief of investigation for the Atchison, Topeka, and Santa Fe, and the man who was probably his oldest and closest friend, he said:

SORRY MISSED YOU CHEYENNE HELD HERE WEEKS YET STOP WHO DO WE KNOW MOP AUSTIN STOP UN-IMPORTANT BUT WISH DO FRIEND FAVOR STOP REPLY USUAL AUSTIN NEXT WEEK.

You could always be suspicious of Johnny Quillen, "Big Q" in the code he and Conrad Meuse employed, especially when Johnny just happened to be passing through. Johnny was up to something. Johnny wanted something. And of course Johnny would be just as suspicious, any time Hewitt worked on anything "unimportant," to do a friend a favor.

It took a certain amount of machine-tool equipment to stamp out fifty-dollar gold counterfeits and then coat them with a gold wash afterward. One good way to run down such equipment was through railway bills of lading. "MOP" meant Missouri Pacific, which served Austin, and indeed the whole of the East Texas piney dunes.

Hate to cut old Johnny in, if this turns out to be a rich one, Hewitt thought, as he got ready to bathe and shave. On the other hand, he wants something of me, or he wouldn't have been to Cheyenne. Maybe we can trade help. Sew up my pockets first, of course. . . .

Shaved and bathed, he locked himself into his room at Mrs. Latimore's, and composed himself for a two-hour nap. The afternoon grew hotter, more humid. The sweat coursed off him as he lay, sleeping silently on his back, and deeply. Jefferson Hewitt disliked both extreme heat and extreme cold, and above all, humid heat. Yet life had taught him to maintain discipline over himself as he would have over a pet puma. Despite the heat and sweat, he slept exactly two hours and awoke refreshed.

CHAPTER TWO

"These are going to be very dear, you know," the agent said, when Hewitt handed him the telegrams. "I'm sorry, Mr. Hewitt, but I have to tell you the truth."

Hewitt smiled. "You don't make the rates," he said. He slapped a mosquito, and then at another. "They ought to make you take out a hunting license for these things."

"They say you get used to them, but I never have, and I've been here for eighteen years. Wires got here before the rails, and I came with them."

The agent switched into the commercial line, and began tapping out the messages. Hewitt could send fairly fast himself, and read a little, too. He waited until all three wires had been dispatched.

"You're a fast operator, aren't you?" he said, as he paid his bill.

"Fairly fast."

"You have a nice touch, too. Easy to read."

"Oh, are you an operator, Mr. Hewitt?"

"Not like you." Hewitt slid two more one-dollar bills to the man. "I could get a reply to one of those, and I'd appreciate getting it as early as possible."

"The minute it comes in."

They parted friends. Hewitt spent a fortune on telegrams. Conrad sometimes complained about their wire bills, but even he realized that there was no substitute for speed. Hewitt stepped out into the sweltering dusk. He had eaten a good supper, and it would be hours before he was sleepy. No use asking what there was to do in this town. He already knew, and it was nothing.

The Gulf of Mexico lay less than fifty miles to the east. The Mexican border was not much farther away than that, to the south. The wide-open Texas that had become familiar to most Americans, through the incredible but still truthful adventure tales that came out of it, lay hundreds of miles to the north and west.

This was a drab little county seat, with nothing of interest here except money. Every evening the town was full of cowboys, although this was not "cattle country" as most cowboys knew it. You could grow anything in this sandy soil, with this heat and humidity. Cattlemen here grew barley and other crops to fatten the cattle they bought off the short-grass range to the north and west. They shipped them from the Gulf ports to the hungry cities of the East Coast, and to England and Europe.

And wherever money was made, Jefferson Hewitt found life interesting. The many, many ways people had to make money were fascinating. That he could make as much as he had made, for a lot of years, was one of the wonders that made his own life interesting. To do a good job was a cause for satisfaction, to make money, another. To do both at the same time approached the perfect life.

He strolled down the single main street, and in front of the Lone Star saloon, tipped his hat to Sheriff Bill Wetherly. Bill looked like a sullen, stupid, overbearing country oaf, but in working the forgery case, Hewitt had come to know he was anything but that.

"Just a minute, Mr. Hewitt. Like to talk to you, soon as I'm finished here," the sheriff said.

Hewitt waited until the sheriff had impressed a kid cowboy with the desirability of a reputation for quiet sobriety.

"You're too young to get tanked up this way," Bill said, gripping the kid by the shirt front, and shaking him until his teeth chattered, "but you ain't too young to die. I catch you lapping it up this way again, I'm going to kick your butt clear to Indian Territory."

"I'm gonna be all right now, Sheriff," the kid said, pleadingly. "My legs is still a little drunk, but my head is sober. Just give me a chance."

Bill propped him up against the wall and came to join Hewitt. It had grown darker, and lamps had been lighted all up and down the street.

"Mr. Hewitt, I heard some talk that you wear a forty-five under that coat," the sheriff said. "I reckon you know they's a county ordinance against wearing guns in any populated place."

Hewitt unbuttoned and opened his black frock coat, which he wore despite the steamy heat because it was a caste mark, and in this town, he wanted to look like an important man. "I've been known to wear one, Bill," he said, "but I know the rules of the game."

"I knowed I could count on you."

"May I ask who complained?" When the sheriff shook his head, Hewitt went on, "Not anyone who lives here, surely. I don't think I've made enemies here."

"A stranger complained, when I made him take his'n off, Mr. Hewitt. Everybody in this town knows what you done for the bank, and it's appreciated. People in a cow or farming town, they live or die with the bank," the sheriff said earnestly.

"That makes me feel good," Hewitt said truthfully, as they parted. He ambled onward, puffing on his cigar, keeping a cloud of smoke around his head to ward off the fat but still voracious mosquitoes, and thinking how many times friends had made the difference between winning and losing a case.

He could make friends anywhere, and he knew it. He had cultivated the art of making friends, yet in his heart he was sure it was not the false fawning of a man running for office. You did not have to fawn. Most people had some small distinction or other, and all you had to do was notice and appreciate the one thing that made them different and better. The telegraph operator, for instance. He had a compliment coming, but he had probably gone many a lean year without one.

A clerk in one of the local stores was watching at the window for him. He tapped on the glass for Hewitt to wait, and came out as soon as he could finish with his customer. Hewitt sat next to him at Mrs. Latimore's table, and had made a friend of him, too. His name was Lloyd Gaunt.

"Been back to the house since supper, Mr. Hewitt?"

"No, I haven't, Mr. Gaunt, why?"

"Man there to see you. Very anxious. I told you was heading for the depot, but he said he'd wait. Mrs. Latimore put him in the parlor."

Gaunt had no idea who the man was, nor could he describe him. Hewitt thanked him warmly and turned toward the boarding house.

Doc Nolan was waiting in the parlor. "Oh Jesus, I thought you'd never get here, Mr. Hewitt!" he said, when Hewitt walked into the room. "Listen, I got to have them gold pieces back!"

"Now, wait a minute, Doc—what's this all about?" Hewitt said.

"It's nothing for you to fret about. If you want more, you just go where I told you, and you'll find plenty. I still got all the money you give me. Look, here it is!"

Nolan pulled the wad of currency from his pocket and tried to make Hewitt take it. He refused.

"It's no good, Doc. The minute I hand this back to you, we're both on the wrong side of federal law. Tell me what's bothering you, and let's see if we can't fix it."

"Mr. Hewitt, I can't. I don't dare!"

"You're not getting the coins back."

Something wolfish came into Nolan's dark eyes in the parlor lamplight, and as if by instinct, his hand went to the front of his shirt. Hewitt caught his wrist, found the nerve with his fingertips, and bent the arm back. Nolan was stronger than he looked. They struggled silently, toe to toe, only one arm of each engaged.

Hewitt gouged the nerve again, and Doc twisted and let his arm go limp. Hewitt stepped back.

"Don't try anything like that on me again, Doc. Now, let's talk this over. Why do you want the coins? Do you have to give them back to someone else?"

Nolan rubbed his throbbing wrist and looked down at the floor. "What do you care why I want them back? I'll give you back every cent. That'll leave less than a dollar— and by God, Mr. Hewitt, I don't know where I'm going to sleep tonight, that's how much money means to me."

"No good, Doc. Who wants the coins?" Doc did not answer. Hewitt prodded him, "You can sleep here. I'll feed you until we get this straightened out. Don't bother to lie to me. Somebody wants them back, that's plain. Who?"

"Nobody you know," Doc said reluctantly.

"I intend to know him. Does he know who has them?"

No answer. Hewitt looked Nolan over carefully. The man was not a coward, but he was in mortal terror now. Why? No ordinary threat could turn the soft, smooth, cynical man who had thumbnailed the pinochle deck just for

fun, into this pallid, sick, and confused quiverer. Some
men were terrified of snakes—Johnny Quillen, for one. Big
Q was big, tough, cool, a real beast in a fight. But show
him a fifteen-inch garter snake and he babbled and
vomited.

Something, or someone, had terrified Nolan that way.
Hewitt was tempted to help the man; but not much. Give
in to that kind of terror, and it always came back. You
did a man no favor to collaborate in his cowardice.

He pushed Doc out of the parlor and then out the front
door. "You're not going to get them back and you may as
well forget it and come play some pinochle," he told Doc.
"As long as you're with me, nothing's going to happen."

Doc believed him for a few minutes. At the first lighted
store, he turned without a word and scuttled back the way
he had come. Hewitt looked about for whatever had startled
the little man, and saw nothing.

Whatever it is, he decided, he can't face it, poor little
man. . . . Hewitt knew what it was to be afraid, although
he had never felt the kind of quaking, eerie terror that had
hold of Doc Nolan. The scares Hewitt remembered all had
helped teach him to stay sure-footed and ready to attack.
The only safe time to run, really, was when the other fellow
expected you to do something else.

He headed for the courthouse and, he hoped, another
pinochle game. They never seemed to play partners in this
town. Always three-handed, every man for himself. Well,
if that was the way they liked it. . . .

There were few "strange" towns to Jefferson Hewitt.
Not just his ability to make friends, but the very life he led,
made it possible for him to settle into a town like a broody
hen settling down on a clutch of eggs. His beat was the entire western half of the United States. He came and went

like a perpetual outcast, yet was at home everywhere. This was why he got so many telegrams, so few letters.

Jefferson Hewitt was a man of many skills and no genius. Born in the Missouri Ozarks, he was fifteen years old, and almost illiterate, when he joined the Army. Five years as a soldier had been his school and college. He had seen at once the disadvantage of his lack of education, and had set about educating himself as fast as possible.

He never rose higher than corporal, but this was only because he had learned, very early, the opportunities that went with being company clerk. He was not just a good company clerk—many an officer swore that he was the best in the Army.

He worked for the Pinkerton agency after leaving the Army, first on the Oakland docks, where he quickly broke a huge, rich robbery ring that was driving the shippers crazy. He found he had a talent for detective work. Young as he was, he was sure of himself, personable, convincing. Impatient to be done with a job and get paid for it, he probably gave more thought to the work than most field operatives. It made him, very early in life, a crafty operative.

He worked a few divorce cases and was very good at them, because besides being young and virile-looking, he never lost his head over a woman. But he was still better in cases involving livestock, because of his rural background. Even as a barefoot kid, he had been a hard man to fool on a critter; and this talent, too, he cultivated.

Apparently he had been born with a knack for copying "pitchers," as he called them then. He developed this into a respectable skill with pencil, crayons, or paints, and while he knew he would never be truly an artist, he could have made his living at the graphic arts somehow.

A physician that he had sent to jail had taught him about muscles, bones, and the connecting tissues, so that

Hewitt was an expert masseur. He had cracked two cases by merely giving certain key people "treatments" that magically relieved them of headaches.

He had been a good shot when he went into the Army. He came out of it a better one, and today was better still. He was not as good as his reputation—no man is that good —but he did nothing to discourage the gossip. He was said to have killed eleven, or nine, or eight, or thirteen men. Actually he had killed four, when there was no way out of killing, and had never lost an hour's sleep over it.

He was a student of American accents, and could imitate enough of them to get by even among the natives who spoke them. He would never forget one evening in eastern Tennessee, when he was looking for a murderer for whom there had been a $2,000 reward. "Where you been the last year, mister?" he was asked. "You been away from Tinnessee a spell, I kin tell that on you." It was an accolade that still pleased him, when he thought of it.

He did not mind that people hated private detectives. He quit the Pinkertons only because a Cheyenne, Wyoming, bank offered to finance him and another man in a partnership. Hewitt had never met Conrad Meuse until they were introduced at the bank. They took a liking to each other, and no doubt each respected the other's good, healthy avarice.

Hewitt now worked out of his own Cheyenne office, and was a full partner in Bankers' Bonding & Indemnity Company. Conrad did the bonding of clerks, treasurers, and other officials and employees required to put up surety. Hewitt did the field investigative work, not merely on the bonding jobs, but on the criminal cases that took up most of his time.

Hewitt liked to live well. He knew the best hotels in most cities, and he could order a meal with wine and without *gaucherie.* He spoke bad Spanish fluently, better than average German, and enough French to carry on a simple conversation.

He liked women. He was successful with women, but he was pretty sure he had never hurt one. He had thought of marriage, but not very seriously.

He was a good gambler, and twice had made gambling a cover for his investigation. He could always go back to gambling, if some physical disability cost him his career as a detective.

If pressed, Hewitt would admit that he believed in God, but he would never discuss religion with anyone. He had prayed at a few deathbeds, but never for anything for himself. Under the deal he had struck with his God, he used the strengths and skills he had been given with gratitude, but he asked no favors.

He was a rich man, because Conrad Meuse handled their money and was as good at this one thing as Hewitt was at all his manifold scattered talents. Someday he expected to retire, and perhaps even get married. But not yet.

Dory Ketchum's wife had put her foot down; so the county clerk's office was closed, and tonight they played in the big bullpen cell in Sheriff Bill Wetherly's jail. They had started with three separate games, but by midnight a sort of tournament play-off had developed. There was one game going, and a cellful of watchers.

Jefferson Hewitt was one of the players. The other two were an undertaker and a general insurance broker. "To be a good card player is to be a bum and a loafer in this town," the undertaker said to Hewitt. "Ollie and me, now—our business makes us experts, you might say, at calculating the odds. It gives us a bidding philosophy, you might say. What's your excuse?"

"Oh, I just like to beat the hell out of philosophers," said Hewitt.

He did not particularly care for pinochle after it became too toughly competitive. It was a good game to pass time with, but it was too unscientific, and too dependent on the fall of the cards, to risk his reputation on a playoff. The cards had been falling his way, but he was glad when Bill Wetherly came pushing into the office.

Bill did not often allow them to play in his jail—just often enough, in fact, to keep the men content, without making their wives mad. One of these times, Bill believed, Dory Ketchum was going to make Eloise so damn mad, the way he stayed out all night to play pinochle, she'd see he got beat at the next election.

"Mr. Hewitt, could I see you a minute?"

Hewitt got up and went into Bill's private office with him. They did not sit down.

"Want you to come look at a dead body," Bill said.

Hewitt raised his eyebrows. "Anybody I know?"

"Clothes look like somebody you might. Lloyd Gaunt— I reckon you know Lloyd—he works at Neill's Market and lives at Phyllis Latimore's—"

"I know Lloyd, yes," Hewitt said uneasily.

"Lloyd said he thought this feller was the one that came to see you at Mrs. Latimore's. Sure as hell ain't going to be no other way to identify him. I seen a few dead men, but this is the horriblest yet."

They slipped out without drawing the pinochle crowd after them. Someone taking a short cut home between two buildings had tripped over the body in the dark, and had come out shrieking bloody murder. Late as it was, there were still a dozen men gathered at the scene of the crime, several of them holding lanterns.

The sheriff took one lantern and handed it to Hewitt.

Hewitt leaned over, shaking his head. He could understand the sheriff's queasy look; he felt sick himself.

The man had been literally cut to pieces, and probably beaten besides. Any of more than two dozen wounds would have caused death, Hewitt was sure. The knife that had been used lay in the dirt beside the body.

"Has the knife been removed from his body by anyone, or is that where it was found?" he asked.

"Why, what difference does it make?" said Bill.

"Maybe none, but it's his own knife. I saw it this evening."

"You do know him, then. Who is he?"

"I know one name for him. It may be his own—it probably is, in fact—but I imagine he has used others. I think we had better sit down somewhere and talk about this, Sheriff, and it might be a good idea to get Dory Ketchum over, too. That's where I met this fellow."

The three of them talked it over far into the night, in Bill's private office. Dory Ketchum had known the man as John W. Simmons, land title expert, possibly one of the sharks who sought out defective titles and filed nuisance suits. He might even, Dory thought, be an investor himself.

"He's been here three days now, mostly going over bond and tax records. Now, here's the funny thing, Bill. He kept nice and neat and clean, but I see him coming out of the schoolhouse early one morning, and I just wondered at the time if the poor devil wasn't so broke he had to sleep there. I never seen him eat much."

Bill looked at Hewitt, who gave him a significant look back before saying, carefully, "That certainly doesn't conflict with anything I knew about him. I had quite a talk with him this afternoon, but I never saw him before today."

Bill sent Dory home. When he and Hewitt were alone,

Hewitt told him all he knew about the man he had known as Eoain B. "Doc" Nolan. He showed him the three brass slicks with the gold wash on them. He showed him the receipt that Nolan had written at his dictation.

"What do you want with these?" Bill said, tapping the gold pieces with a thick forefinger.

"I work for a living. This is the way I make my cases."

"You can spare one, can't you? In case any more of them turn up around here."

"Help yourself."

"You say you paid this bird two hundred dollars."

"Yes. Alf Hughes saw the transaction."

"Well, Mr. Hewitt, two hundred is what he had on him when he was found."

"The hell you say!"

"The hell I don't. Now this ain't no ordinary kind of a murder, Mr. Hewitt. You got any idees who it was that had the pure hell scared out of him thataway?"

"None—unless you can connect it with whoever it was that accused me of wearing a gun under my coat."

"I was thinking about it along them same lines," Bill said slowly. "Big, tall feller, good shoulders and big hands on him. Well-dressed man, I'd say about forty. Talked like an English lord. You ever talk to an English lord, Mr. Hewitt?"

"Yes. What became of him?"

"Went out of here on the evening train. Reckon I'll have a stir around and try to find out how he arrived here. It just looks to me, now, like he might've stopped off just to do one little job."

Hewitt nodded. "To get those coins back or fix it so no one else would try to get away with any."

"Yes, sir, and do you know what I think? He already knows about you, Mr. Hewitt, or else why would he sic me onto you about wearing a gun? If I's you, I think I'd keep one eye peeled forward and one backward from now on."

"I don't expect to be around here very long myself, unless there's some reason you want me to stay here in connection with this case," said Hewitt.

"You ort to really stay and testify to the coroner's jury, but I don't know anything else to keep you." Bill was silent a moment and unsmiling. "Helping the bank out is just fine, Mr. Hewitt, but murder is something else. I'd purely hate to think you's connected up with any of this."

"I'm not," said Hewitt. "Know what I think?"

"I'd be interested to hear."

"His story to me, of how he got the money, is probably true. When he discovered it was counterfeit, it made him think of something else he knew. Something he wasn't supposed to know. My guess is that his instinct was to throw the slicks away and run like a rabbit, but the poor devil couldn't afford to. He had to unload them somewhere because he needed eating money, and when he did it, he knew somebody would be wanting them back."

"Well, you got a lot more experience with this here kind of s'phisticated crime than I have," Bill said, yawning. "You go at it your way and I'll go at it mine, same as I would a henhouse robbery or somebody's fat calves being run off, or the Clayton-Vasquez feud. All I know to do is look."

"That's all I know, too," said Hewitt.

CHAPTER THREE

The 161 was a big place, but not as big as it had been twenty years ago, before Simon Taylor began paying his son's debts. It looked idle but not rundown, to Hewitt. He tied his horse to the branch of a tree and looked around for signs of life.

The big, low-roofed house had an empty look, and so did the long bunkhouse. A few horses switched their tails in tight, well-kept corrals. Beyond them, the little houses occupied by the families of the Mexican workers were all full, but he saw only women and children about them.

An old man came out of the bunkhouse, yawning and putting on his hat. "Hidy, stranger," he said, stumping toward Hewitt on tired old feet. "Kin I help you?"

"Looking for Mr. Simon Taylor, sir," said Hewitt.

The old man came up to him and looked him over carefully. He appeared to be the typical old stove-in cowboy, who was grateful to the outfit that let him hang around and do chores for a bare living for the rest of his life. Not very bright, surely, or he would not have come to this pass in his old age. Loyalty would be his salient trait.

"I dunno, now," the old man said, scratching his grizzled white whiskers. "Si ain't feeling peart, lately. He don't like to be bothered unless it's important."

Hewitt let the old man see a five-dollar gold piece. "It's important to me, whether it is to him or not," he said. "He could probably save both of us a lot of trouble, if we had a little talk now."

"Tommie owe you money? He won't pay it."

Hewitt kept the gold piece in sight. "No, but tell him Tommie has paid too many bills. That's what I want to talk over with him—the bills Tommie has already paid."

"I dunno, now. Let me see."

The old man shuffled across the bare yard and went in a side door of the house. Hewitt waited in the shade of the tree. A hen came up beside him and waited expectantly to be fed something. Another hen, trailed by a dozen week-old chicks, waited a little way away.

Patience, patience, Hewitt told himself. . . . He had no client and was spending partnership money. He still had most of the five hundred dollars that Conrad had wired to him, but it would not last forever. Doc Nolan's story had been vague and inconclusive, and Hewitt already had two weeks of work invested in a job on which he had not the promise of a penny's pay. Bankers' Bonding & Indemnity Company, Cheyenne, did not often speculate either money or time.

Nevertheless, Hewitt could smell money, and there had been nothing vague or inconclusive about those slick fifty-dollar gold pieces. He could only hope that the Treasury so far had no lead on the case. So long as Secret Service had a hope of solving their own cases, free-lance efforts were regarded as interference. You had to catch them early, and break their hearts by notifying them of a fresh counterfeiting scheme, or wait until it had gone on and on and on regardless of their best efforts.

These coins were far from perfect, but they were good enough to get into wide circulation, and they had been made by a method that could turn out millions of dollars' worth of them. The very credit of the United States might be endangered, unless the stream of those machine-made slicks could be dammed up. This was a far more dangerous scheme than the counterfeiting of paper currency. Make a nation's gold questionable, and you struck at its heart.

The old man came to the front door and crooked a finger at Hewitt. "Si says he can't fool around with you more than a minute or two, but come on in."

Hewitt went into a big, square living room that did not look like anybody's home. There was a sheeted grand piano, and tables with dust on them deep enough to hide their color. The bare pine floors had been recently scrubbed with lye water, but the rugs had not been put back down. The woman who had been mistress of this house had been dead a long time, and not even a ghost remained.

The old flunky pointed, and Hewitt went on through into the kitchen, and then into another room behind it. An old man sat in a barber chair, an apron around him. A Mexican woman in her middle years was snipping at the sides of his white hair. His head was bald on top and very clean. He had been freshly shaven this morning.

"What's on your mind, stranger?" he said. His frosty blue eyes stayed on Hewitt watchfully, although his voice was gentle and reasonably polite.

"I picked up some gold coins recently. You probably know what I'm talking about. I want to find out where they came from." When the old man said nothing, Hewitt went on softly, "Before the Treasury starts looking. They never know when to stop, you know."

"How would I know anything about it?"

"Now, Mr. Taylor, if we have to waste time like this, you can't help me and I can't help you, can I?"

The old man continued to glower at him silently a moment. He sat up straight, and motioned for the woman to hand him a mirror. She did so, and then held another so he could study the back of his head.

The job seemed to satisfy him. He dismissed her with a nod, a wave of his hand, and sat up straighter and crossed his legs. Hewitt knew he was at least seventy, but he did not look it now. There was still great strength in his bulky old body, and his mind was sharp. He waited until the woman had gathered up her barber's tools and gone out.

"I guess you seen my son," he said harshly. "I guess you figger to cash in on me. Well, guess again, then! Even if he goes to the pen, I won't lift a hand to help him. So you and me is just wasting time, ain't we?"

Hewitt reached into his pocket for one of the slick fifties. "I haven't seen your son," he said, "but this came from him. He swiped it from you. You've got quite a collection of these beauties left, and they cost you a big chunk of real money. How would you like to get it back?"

"Throw good money after bad, you mean. No, I'll take my loss. Who are you?"

Hewitt handed him a business card for Bankers' Bonding & Indemnity Company. "I don't usually speculate on a job, Mr. Taylor, but this one is big enough to make the risk worthwhile. I want a third of everything we recover from the man who sold these to you. That's expensive to you, but cheaper than taking your loss."

"Suppose he's already spent it?"

"There is pretty sure to be some money. I don't know if you know anything about the counterfeiting game—"

"I don't know anything."

"I'll try to tell you about it, then. Whoever made these has quite an investment in dies and equipment. He's not going to be satisfied to dribble a few of them out here and there. He has to move big amounts of money to make the job worth all the risk and investment.

"The bulk of this counterfeit would probably be put into circulation in Mexico. Before he moves into that phase of his plan, he can't risk putting any of this coinage into circulation. He's already in bad trouble. He had to kill a man, trying to get a few coins back. He didn't get them. I rather think that he'll have to change his plans a little, now.

"I think your deal with him probably provided him with enough money for emergencies. It's the last deal he'll make, until he goes for the big killing. That has to be at least a million dollars' worth of these coins, maybe more. But he won't spend any more of your good money than he has to. This will be his emergency getaway fund.

"The signs are that he went broke, which is why he made a deal with you in the first place. That isn't going to happen to him a second time. No, there'll be some good money hidden around somewhere. All we have to do is find it before the Treasury does."

"I see. S'pose you did run into somebody that had a whole lot of this false money, is he going to have to go to prison for it? On top of taking his loss, I mean."

"He's going to have to give up the coins. He'll probably have to testify. But as long as we've still got the coins, we're in a position to bargain."

"You say 'we,' like you's already in."

"Well, if I'm not," Hewitt said with a smile, "then I'm afraid you'll have to bargain with the Treasury yourself. I think you'd be a lamb bargaining with a wolf, Mr. Taylor."

Taylor thought it over. "It's about noon. You et yet, Mr. Hewitt? Let's you and me set down and break bread together and see if we can't work something out."

They had finished eating, but were still at the table, when the woman who had cut Taylor's hair came in and put a small leather satchel on the table. She went out without a word. The servant came in with the coffeepot, and refilled their cups. Taylor waited until she had gone, too.

"There's your brass money, Mr. Hewitt," he said, with a nod toward the satchel. "Make the best deal you can for me with the gov'ment and you can have a third of all you get back of my money."

Hewitt unbuckled the straps that closed the satchel, and took out the muslin bag inside. He loosened its drawstring enough to expose the coins and verify that they were exactly like the ones he had got from Doc Nolan. He retied the bag, put it back in the valise, and buckled the straps again.

"Better put that away again, Mr. Taylor," he said.

"I thought you wanted it."

"When it comes time to make a deal, I do. Better make some arrangement so I can get it when I need it, if anything happens to you. Until then, let's just let everyone wonder where it is."

"Tommie knows I've got it. That's my son."

"But they still have to find it and prove you own it. Mr. Taylor, I want this coin out of circulation as badly as the Treasury. It's my country, too. But what I don't want to see happen is for them to make a hash of the case, and put somebody on trial just to get a conviction. You, for instance. Now, tell me how you got this stuff."

"You ain't going to believe it, Mr. Hewitt."

Taylor leaned back in his chair, coffee cup in hand, and told Hewitt his story. He had been in New Orleans, to close a deal for some railroad shares he owned, and after closing it, had got to drinking with some men in the hotel bar. He was not worried about getting drunk enough to lose his money. He had taken payment for the shares in a check that was made out to his Texas bank, for deposit to his

account. No way he could have cashed it anywhere but
at that bank.

He rarely got drunk, but he did this time. He woke up in
his own room in the hotel about noon the next day with
the usual hangover misery. It was the middle of the afternoon before he was in shape to make a judgment about
anything. By then, he knew he had lost his check somewhere. Apparently he had cashed one of his own somewhere, too, because he had more than two hundred dollars
in his pockets.

He managed to get some food down, in the hotel dining
room, and keep it there. He was just heading back for his
room and more sleep, when a man who somehow looked
familiar accosted him.

"Wait a minute," said Hewitt. "Suppose you describe him
to me, will you?"

"Six-footer, eyes gray or blue, medium-brown hair,
prob'ly about forty years old and a mean son of a bitch to
tangle with, would be my guess. Englishman."

Hewitt was not surprised. It was probably the same one
who had tipped Sheriff Bill Wetherly to search him for
a gun. Find him, Hewitt decided, and you were not far
from whoever ran the counterfeiting business. He nodded
to Taylor to go on.

"Excuse me," the stranger said to Taylor. "I'm sure
you're not in any shape for neighborly gossip today, but I
wanted to turn this over to you. You were doing your best
to give it away last night."

It was the check for Taylor's shares of stock, in the
amount of $11,485.10. Taylor took it gratefully. Before
he could mumble his thanks, the stranger offered him some
currency. "You played some very bold poker last night," he
said smilingly, "and you can probably be grateful that you

became ill in time. I wonder if you remember asking me to take care of your winnings for you, eh?"

Blearily, he did remember something like that. He could even recall the poker game, which took place in the Englishman's room. He might even remember being helped back to his own room by the Englishman and somebody else.

He stuffed the money into his pocket, managed to thank the Englishman, and tottered back to his room. "To make a long story short, but no less foolish," Taylor said, "I talked to the desk clerk, and he told me I'd cashed a check for three hundred dollars. I got every cent of it back from this Englishman and was better than two hundred dollars to the good. He could've took every cent, and I would never knowed the difference. I know now that he done that, just so I'd trust him later on."

Hewitt restrained a chuckle and nodded sympathetically. Taylor just happened to run into the stranger the next day. His name, it turned out, was Edgar Erickson, and he owned a plantation, called "Randsburg," a hundred miles up the river. A single man, he knew a number of charming women in New Orleans. It just happened that he was going out to dinner with one that night. Her sister would be going along, and if Mr. Taylor cared . . .

Mr. Taylor cared. Sometime in the course of a lovely evening, one of the ladies just happened to ask Mr. Erickson when he was going to Mexico. Unfortunately, not for a while, said the Englishman, and it disturbed him greatly because he was letting a very dear friend down. The friend was Hector Sámana, a wealthy cattleman and rancher in San Luis Potosí.

"Hector Sámana?" Taylor exclaimed. "Why, me and Hector has been friends for thirty years!"

It was indeed a small world. Taylor delayed his return

to Texas to talk more about old Hector. It seemed that Mr. Erickson had a friend who owned a California gold mine. He could not file on it because it was on someone else's land, and to have shipped gold to the mint would have caused him to lose it and the mine too. Wherefore he had arranged to strike it into coins himself and move them through Mexico.

The counterfeiter had invested a lot of time and money in the coins—that, Hewitt already knew. He had invested still more in setting Taylor up for the kill, to lay his hands on some real American money in large quantities. Hewitt almost had to admire him for his persistence, patience, and imagination.

"Actually, the coins are each worth a dollar or two more than the ones that our own government mints, so no one can possibly lose anything by taking them in. I'm sure that the Treasury eventually will buy them all up and make a tidy little profit out of protecting the coinage. Meanwhile, though, they can be bought for twenty cents on the dollar. I managed to get a thousand of them for Hector," Erickson said.

"That's fifty thousand dollars," Taylor gulped. He must have been beady-eyed and wet of palm with greed, by then.

Erickson smiled. "Yes, but of course he paid only ten thousand for them. Or will, when I collect from him. There is really no hurry, except that—well, you know Hector! Delightful man, but what's his, he wants in his own hand."

Taylor had to swallow several times. "Wouldn't mind getting in on a proposition like that myself."

He asked for it. They always did, if the right man used the right technique in appealing to avarice in them. Taylor lingered another day in New Orleans, while Erickson investigated the possibility of getting coins for him. As things turned out, it would take at least a month.

But Erickson had a solution for the problem. "Why don't you take Hector's coins?" he asked. "When I get more in, I'll deliver them to you at your place in Texas. You can take your own down when you deliver Hector's to him, and turn them into good American coinage. We can't get Hector's to him any sooner, and meanwhile, you know you're getting yours."

Ready to double-cross even his friend Hector Sámana, Taylor agreed. They went to a New Orleans bank, which wired to Taylor's bank for confirmation, and then cashed his check for ten thousand dollars. Taylor gave Erickson the money.

That same afternoon, Erickson delivered the coins in the leather satchel that Hewitt had seen. Erickson took a handful of them out in Taylor's room, so he could examine them before turning over the ten thousand dollars.

"Mr. Hewitt, I may be a sucker but I ain't that kind of a damn fool. I can tell real gold! What he showed me was gold. You couldn't tell it from the official coinage, for the damn good reason that it *was* official coinage! He slipped them out of his sleeve, prob'ly, when he dipped his hand into the satchel. I paid him off, and that's the last I saw of him," Taylor said.

Half an hour later, he locked the door of his room and prepared to gloat over his wonderful homemade gold. He took the muslin bag out, untied it, and emptied it on the bed. He knew instantly that he had been made the victim of a high-power confidence game, and he had no one to blame but himself.

He stuck his .45 in the belt of his pants and spent a week looking for Erickson. There was a plantation called "Randsburg," but it was owned by the Rand family and always had been. The bank that had cashed Taylor's check had carried a small savings account for Mr. Edgar Erickson; it had

never risen higher than fifty dollars, and had been cleaned
out the morning that "Erickson" delivered the slicks to
Taylor.

Taylor could not find the men he had played poker with,
nor the two lovely ladies who had accompanied him and
Erickson to dinner. Things came back to him little by little,
though, as he prowled the streets of New Orleans with a
.45 under his belt and blind fool's fury in his heart. For
one thing, he could remember that one of the poker players
had been from San Luis Potosí, and that he had not been
surprised when it turned out that the fellow knew his old
friend Hector Sámana.

"It's no use pointing out that a con game is built on the
easy mark's willingness to make money illegally," said Hewitt, "but it has to be said. You must understand that you're
standing with one foot on a round rock and the other one
in a tarantula's nest."

"I know that," Taylor said gloomily. "Make the best deal
you can with the gov'ment. If I got to go to the pen, I won't
mind too much."

"How did your son get his hands on the coins?"

"I had the bag in my hand when I got off the train in
San 'Tone. All I could think was to take it out to my own
property and bury it somewhere. But that son of mine, hon-
est to God, Mr. Hewitt, he could step on a dime with new
boots on, and tell you whether it's heads or tails up! I know
somebody got into it, first night I was home, because twenty
coins was missing when I counted them. You say he paid
three out to somebody. I'd say your first job is to try to get
back however much Tommie has got left."

"Where would I find your son?"

"Try Hobbie's saloon, in San 'Tone. If he ain't there, he'll
be back shortly."

"Mr. Taylor, what's he like?"

Taylor flinched. "I got me a dandy, there. Never would work. Used to be quite a ladies' man, but since he's got older, and can't get at my money to spend, they've lost interest in him. About my build, supposed to look a lot like me, but I be damned if I ever looked as shifty as he does. You don't have to go easy on Tommie for my sake."

"I will anyway, Mr. Taylor," said Hewitt.

He was riding a rented horse that was much better than the average livery-stable mount, and was in San Antonio shortly after dark. He put his horse up and, carrying his light saddle valise, started to look for a hotel.

Hobbie's saloon was less than a block from the stable. Two men were coming out of it, just as Hewitt turned toward the door. One looked so much like Simon Taylor that it was a shock to Hewitt. He let them pass, went in, and found the barroom almost deserted. He leaned against the bar and waited for service.

He downed a whiskey and ordered another to sip. "You like good whiskey," the bartender observed. "It's a pleasure to serve your brand, sir."

"Have one yourself," said Hewitt.

The bartender smiled and shook his head. "Thank you, but I never touch it. In this business, when you start sampling your own merchandise, you're on the downhill trail to bankruptcy."

"If you own the place, you must be Mr. Hobbie."

"Bart Hobbie, yes, sir."

"Was that Tommie Taylor who just left?"

"Yes. He went quietly tonight. He don't always."

"Any idea where I might find him?"

"He'll be at home. Nothing for Tommie to do but read, when he's this broke. That's none of my put-in, of course.

Only, Tommie's a nasty drunk. Anybody that makes a pest of himself like Tommie, I don't owe him nothing."

"Know the man who was with him?"

"He goes by the name of Sullivan, all I know. They call him Sully. A printer by trade, he claims. Mostly, Sully just drinks."

Hewitt paid for his drinks with a five-dollar gold piece, and left the change on the bar. He also left a friend behind. Hobbie told him how to find the house where Tommie Taylor lived.

"White-painted 'dobe, with a white picket fence around it. Tommie's got a room with an outside door, so he don't have to go through the house to go in and out. If there's anybody waiting in the shadders under the tree that shades that door, he's trying to catch Tommie to make him pay up what he owes him. Tommie owes everybody in town."

The house was less than three blocks away. It was easy to identify from Hobbie's description. Hewitt let himself through the gate in the picket fence silently, carrying his saddle valise. He avoided the path as he headed for the door that led to Tommie's room.

He could hear someone arguing inside—not loudly, but pretty spiritedly. Hewitt stopped under the tree and put his bag down. He listened carefully, but he could make out only a few words in a breathless, moaning voice:

"I didn't, I swear I didn't! You know I been broke for a month. I didn't, I didn't, I didn't."

Hewitt took from his pocket the limber, lead-filled sap that was his favorite weapon, and slid silently toward the door. It opened, and a man came out. It was too dark for Hewitt to recognize him, but he was panting with terror or excitement or both, and he had a gun in his hand.

He never knew what struck him. Hewitt twirled the sap, using the strength of his wrist rather than his arm, and dropped the man on the doorstep. He leaned over, felt of his pulse, and smiled in the dark with pleasure at his own accuracy. Bad headache in the morning, and subject to dizzy spells for a day or two, but otherwise sound.

Hewitt took the gun. He also took the small, cloth tobacco bag that the fellow had in his other hand. He went on into the room and closed the door. It was pitch dark in here. He had to grope his way across the room to the bed. He felt for the man in it, ran his hand over his face, and felt it come away sticky.

He wiped his hand on the man's own clothing before taking out a match. He struck it and took one quick look at Tommie Taylor. He had been pistol-whipped into unconsciousness, but did not seem to be seriously hurt outside of the cuts on his cheekbones. They would leave ugly scars.

Hewitt lighted a lamp before the match went out. He opened the tobacco sack and counted twelve slick fifty-dollar gold pieces. That meant that five were still missing. Hard to believe that Tommie had spent any of them. He had gone home peaceably to read, rather than drink. He was not likely to do that while he was in funds.

Tommy slept on, but he would be awakening soon— before the other man, Hewitt was sure. When I put them to sleep, they stay asleep for a while, he thought happily. . . . He left the lamp on while he opened the door carefully and caught Sully by his coat.

He dragged the unconscious man inside, picked him up, and dropped him on the bed with Tommie Taylor, on the other side of him, next to the wall. He blew out the light and went out, closing the door behind him. He found a hotel a few blocks away, crawled into bed, and was instantly asleep. He did not toss or turn. His was the sleep of a man whose conscience is clear.

In the morning, he disposed of his horse by paying his bill at the stable, and arranging for the horse to be sent back at his expense as soon as a rider could be found going that way. An hour later, he was on the train for Austin.

CHAPTER FOUR

It was hot and humid in Austin, too, when Hewitt arrived there shortly after midnight. He borrowed a large, brown envelope and some glue from the night telegraph operator, and picked a piece of cardboard up off the floor. He glued the fifteen coins he had taken from Sullivan to the cardboard, and then glued another piece of cardboard over them. He put them in the envelope, addressed it to himself, in care of general delivery, and applied plenty of stamps.

The return delivery address he put on the envelope, with an "After Thirty Days" prefix, was Bankers' Bonding & Indemnity Company, Cheyenne. If he needed the coins in the next thirty days, he could pick them up here at the post office. If he did not pick them up, they would be returned to him at his own office. Meanwhile, he was free of them.

He walked to the hotel, carrying his small valise. He was tired, but he nevertheless felt buoyant and eager. He had a hunch that there was real money in this counterfeiting case, and that Austin was the place to start on it. For one thing the tall man with good shoulders, who talked like an English lord, had taken a train that would bring him here, if he stayed on it all the way.

And why not? Austin was more and more the center of things. San Antonio was still larger, and the Gulf cities were growing fantastically. But the new capitol building under construction in Austin, as well as the new university,

were not mere bait to lure growth and vitality. They meant
that growth and vitality had already arrived.

The Condon House was a new hotel that had not caught
on because it awed the legislators from the range country.
It served wine in its dining room, and aged beef and exotic
pastries. The average Texas legislator wanted whiskey,
fresh-killed beef, and raisin pie. The Condon House's sur-
vival was proof to Hewitt that Austin's future would be
more sophisticated than its past had been.

His large suitcase had arrived and was in storage for
him. His favorite second-floor room had been reserved, and
there were three telegrams in his box at the desk. He read
them before going up to his room. The first was from Denny
McGucken of the Treasury Department. It said:

> SEND ME YOUR INFO IF ANY STOP INCLINED
> TO DISCREDIT ENTIRE RUMOR REGARDS

Hewitt smiled, knowing Denny. McGucken would not
have wired if he was in a mood to discredit stories. He probably had had reports of counterfeit coins *already in circulation,* and hoped to extract as much information from
Hewitt as possible without yielding any himself.

No, if Denny was unworried, he would have written
a short note and saved the government the price of a wire.
If he *was* worried, it wasn't over one or two hand-made
fifties. Denny had good reason to be greatly concerned, if
he had evidence—or even rumors—of coins that could be
made in large quantities. I'm on the right track, Hewitt
thought. There's only one such slick fifty in existence. . . .

The next telegram, from his partner, Conrad Meuse,
was slightly more informative:

> CLUE TO WHAT STOP BIG Q HERE THREE DAYS
> LEFT WITHOUT WORD TO ME STOP RECALL HEY-

WOOD CASE SAME GUMSHOE IN OFFICE SAY HELLO
STOP RETURNED TODAY TOO STOP WHO IS OUR
CLIENT

So Johnny Quillen, who only happened to be passing
through Cheyenne, had lingered there three days! When he
left without checking back with Conrad, it probably meant
that Hewitt's wire to him had been forwarded to Cheyenne.
It was clear now that Johnny was not just making a friendly
social call in Cheyenne.

The Heywood case had involved the will of a deceased
Montana cattleman. Part of the estate consisted of $90,000
in currency, of which $15,000 was in counterfeit hundred-
dollar bills. Pretty fair counterfeits, too, except that they
all had the same bogus serial number. The deceased Heywood had been too smart to be taken in that way; which
meant that somebody had substituted the bad money for
good, making off with $15,000 that belonged to the estate.

In running down the thief, Hewitt had worked with
a Secret Service man by the name of Emmett Lewayne.
Now Hewitt knew that Denny McGucken had more than
offhand interest in the slick fifties. If Emmett came to the
office twice, just to say hello, the inference was clear that
he was remaining in Cheyenne on orders to find out whatever he could about Hewitt.

The last wire, of course, was from Johnny Quillen:

SORRY SAY HAVE NO MOP CONNECTIONS STOP WILL
BE MY OFFICE NEXT THIRTY DAYS STOP IMPOS-
SIBLE LEAVE DESK STOP CALL ON ME IF CAN
HELP ANY OTHER WAY.

The only inference Hewitt could draw from this was
that the whole thing had to be a lie. Now and then, it was
true, competition between railroads grew into downright

hostility, involving people at every level in both companies. This happened so rarely that it was ridiculous for Johnny to pretend he could not refer Hewitt to a Missouri Pacific protection man. No, the only conclusion to be drawn from Johnny's wire was that he would *not* be at his desk in his office for the next thirty days.

Hewitt went up to his room, following an elderly bellboy creaking under his two bags. He tipped the old man a dollar and a half, and sent him out for a quart of good bourbon whiskey. He had one drink, and then the luxury of a hot bath in a real tub. One more drink, and he was ready for bed.

Hewitt usually wore two guns, a .38 in a shoulder holster, and a .45 in a holster he had made himself. It clipped to his belt in front, under his trousers, where he could reach it without unbuttoning his coat. He unloaded the .45 and left it on the dresser, but slept with the .38 under his pillow. The Condon House was as safe as a hotel could be, but it was his practice to take no chances.

He slept the sleep of the just, and was in the hotel dining room for breakfast at seven. He had a favorite table here, facing the door that opened into the lobby, with his back to the wall. Usually, the captain of waiters held it for him for all meals, but the man had no way of knowing Hewitt had checked in.

He had to take another table, his favorite one being occupied by a woman dawdling at her breakfast alone. Hewitt sat where he could not help seeing her. As he drank his coffee, waiting for his steak and eggs to be served, he watched her with growing interest.

Not a girl, but a mature woman—say, thirty to thirty-five. Rather small and slight, with an undistinguished figure. Hair light brown, and lots of it, worn in some sort of soft arrangement under one of the ugliest hats Hewitt had ever seen. Her face was absolutely enchanting, with the clearest skin, and eyes of the deepest blue. When she smiled her thanks at the waiter, she displayed two captivating dimples.

He liked a woman who ate heartily, and she had a thick piece of ham on her plate, with grits and red gravy. She ate slowly, quite daintily, but she ate every bite. When she had signed the check and got up to go, he liked her sedate little suit of green linen immensely.

His eyes followed her part of the way across the room, liking the natural grace of her fast walk, which had nothing of the studied artfulness of the actress. If only she had not worn that God-awful hat!

He forgot her as he worked that morning. He visited three banks, and talked to the president of each. He identified himself by presenting a letter Alf Hughes had written for him. The conversation thereafter was almost identical in all three cases.

"Nice to know you, Mr. Hewitt. Alf Hughes is a good friend of mine, as well as a good banker. I will be most happy to help you, in any way I can."

"First, I wonder if you have seen any of these coins," showing them the fifty-dollar slick.

"This is counterfeit, you know, Mr. Hewitt."

"I know. That's why I'm here."

"Not the best counterfeit in the world, but I'm sure it could be passed. It even looks like real gold."

"It is real gold, on the outside. That's what's called a jeweler's wash. I'm sure it's brass inside."

"Are there many of these in circulation?"

"I don't think so. There will be millions in the near future, I'm afraid, if we don't put them out of business."

"Who do you mean by 'we,' Mr. Hewitt?"

"My client and I. I'll co-operate with the Secret Service, of course, but so far, I haven't been able to interest them."

"I see. Where are these coins being made?"

"Right here in Austin is a good possibility. I just don't know any more than that. One other question, if I may. I'm trying to locate and identify a tall, athletic man of about forty, who speaks with an upper-class British accent. His hands are large enough to have attracted the attention of at least one person. That's all I have on him. I wonder if you know anyone who fits that much."

They did not, and all three pointed out that anyone with an upper-class British accent would rather stand out in Austin at this time of year. When the legislature was sitting, all sorts of people turned up.

"I'll be at the Condon House, and I'll appreciate it very much indeed, if you'll let me know if one of these bad fifties turn up—or if you have a call from this fellow with the accent and the big hands," Hewitt said as he got up to go.

Two of the bankers agreed. The third said, a little stiffly, that he did not feel he could promise to betray a man who came in to do ordinary business with the bank, just because he had a British accent. "After all," he said, "I don't know you, Mr. Hewitt, or why you want to find this man. I may find I have maligned a perfectly innocent man."

"Let's hope so. I understand completely," Hewitt said with a smile. "I think I should tell you, though, that the last man I know who had contact with his lordship was found dead immediately afterward. Very dead! He was cut to pieces with his own knife."

"I'll let you know if he turns up here, Mr. Hewitt. I don't think we would want him for a client anyway," the banker said.

Hewitt returned to the hotel, just in case there was a new telegram or some other message for him. There was noth-

ing. He thanked the clerk at the desk, and turned toward
the stairs.

He was just in time to collide with a woman coming
down them. He had to catch her arm to keep her from falling, and he could not take off his hat until he had let go
of the arm. He did so, feeling awkward and graceless. It
was the lovely little woman he had seen at breakfast.

"I'm so sorry! That was clumsy of me," he said.

"That's quite all right," she said, in the tone of voice that
meant it was anything but all right. The blue eyes snapped
angrily before she turned away.

She gave a little cry, and almost fell again. He had to
jump to catch her. "Are you hurt, ma'am?" he said.

"It's only my foot. A cramp, I'm afraid. Please think
nothing of it. It will go away."

"Let me help you to a chair, madam."

"It is nothing. Please don't bother."

But when she put her foot down, she had to close her
eyes with pain. Hewitt put his arm around her and walked
her across the lobby to the nearest chair before she could
object, carrying most of her weight on his arm. She wore a
heavy, musky perfume of some kind, as well as that same
hat. The scent became her—the hat did not.

She looked up at him from the chair. "I broke a bone in
this foot as a child. This isn't serious. It will go away in a
moment."

"May I help you to the dining room, ma'am?"

"You are very kind, thank you, but I'm quite all right."

She looked away, dismissing him politely but firmly. And
the hell with you, too, ma'am, he thought. . . . Going up
the stairs to the second floor, he met the elderly bellboy
coming down.

"Wonder if you can tell me the name of the lady sitting
there," Hewitt said, feeding him a dollar bill.

The old man took it deftly. "You bet! That's Mrs. Chaney, sir. She stays here every time she's in Austin."

On his tour of the banks this morning, Hewitt had noticed a nameplate at a physician's office, Dr. Lowell Chaney. "The doctor's wife?" he said.

"No, but her husband came from the same family. I don't know much about her."

Hewitt went on to the stairs. He kept going until he knew he would be out of sight of anyone in the lobby. He came back quietly, hat in hand, and stepped into an open doorway from which he could watch the lobby.

He was just in time to see Mrs. Chaney get up and go to the dining room. There was no sign of a limp in her swift, graceful walk. Hewitt went thoughtfully to his room, where he washed. He was hungry, and well he might be, since it was after one o'clock. And I'll bet she's starved, he thought, waiting all that time to waylay me. . . .

He went downstairs again, noticing as he came down how wide the staircase was, and how hard it would be for two people to bump together at the bottom. He could have marched a corporal's squad down them and across the lobby without interfering with anyone.

He stopped at the desk and asked for six plain envelopes, without the hotel's return on them. The clerk had to go to a storage closet to get them.

Behind most hotel desks hung a ring of master keys that fit all the guest rooms, housekeeper's storage closets, and sample and conference rooms. Hewitt ducked behind the desk, found the keys where he expected to find them, and dropped them in his pocket. He was studying the register from the other side of the desk when the clerk returned with his six plain envelopes. The register showed him that Mrs. Chaney was in 205. That would be the end room on the same side of the hall as Hewitt's, which was 201.

He tipped the clerk a dollar for the envelopes, and went back upstairs. He had the hall to himself. He went straight to the end of the hall, sorting keys as he went. He had the right key in his hand when he reached 205. He went in and closed and locked the door behind him.

Two small valises, brand new, were on the rack at the foot of the bed, but when he opened them, they were empty. In the closet hung five brand-new dresses and two suits; under them stood six pairs of brand-new boots and shoes.

He opened the drawers of the bureau. Brand-new underwear and stockings, too, and a brand-new kit containing five perfume essences. He sniffed them, one at a time. One was the musky perfume she was wearing now.

Either she bought all new things somewhere, or she hit Austin pink-naked, he thought. He estimated that clothing, suitcases, and perfumes had cost at least two hundred dollars. All very interesting, since she had gone out of her way to contrive an early meeting with him. But why?

He found what he was looking for under the stack of filmy underwear. It was a letter postmarked from Atchison, Kansas, two weeks ago, and it was addressed in a strong, regular handwriting that he knew very well indeed:

Dear M.P.—

Oliver Laverty will give you $400 cash, on your signature, and it will have to do you. No need to account for it to the penny but don't waste it because there won't be any more.

Your pay will be $12 a day, extremely good on top of such generous expenses, you know they don't like to employ women at this work.

Now, this job is very tricky. Subject smart and experienced, not an easy mark for women. Be careful,

*but you haven't got forever, either. I will keep in touch
with the doctor, you use Monty to send messages to
me. Will be thirty minutes away, at the most. Good
luck, but must again urge you to use your head.*

S.F.

Well well, so old Johnny has called in a lady operative
on me, and is making the Missouri Pacific pay her wages!
And cheating her, too, if she's any good; surely it's worth
more than twelve bucks a day to bamboozle me, Hewitt
told himself. . . . The "S.F." signature surely meant the
Santa Fe, for which Johnny worked; what could the "M.P."
salutation mean but Missouri Pacific? And Johnny had
regretted to Hewitt that he knew no one there!

Oliver Laverty had been one of the bankers that Hewitt
had talked to this morning. Beyond doubt, his books would
show a $400 draft from Johnny, with instructions to pay it
on demand to Mrs. Chaney. It was not likely that Laverty
would know the things Hewitt wanted to know—or would
tell him if he did.

The woman was still in the dining room, no doubt, waiting for him to arrive, so she could stage some other plausi-
ble meeting with him. Let her wait! Hewitt went out and
down the stairs. He distracted the clerk's attention long
enough to toss the keys down behind the desk, and went
out the street door. He ate in a neighborhood saloon, and
was lucky enough to run into an old-timer around Austin
who could, and would, tell him what he wanted to know.

Mrs. Chaney's father had been Cornelius Dempsey, edi-
tor and teacher. He was dead now. There would be no
monuments raised to him; yet he had been influential in
more ways than one, always for the good. His wife had
died when the girl, Viola, was only a child. He had brought

her up himself, in his own mold—a pioneer, a crusader for better schools and cleaner politics.

Viola Dempsey was eighteen, and in college in St. Louis, when her father stopped to see her on his way to New York. With him was one of the new state senators he had been influential in electing, Bateman Chaney, who owned a cattle ranch near San Angelo. Chaney was more than twice Viola's age, but they were married the next summer. Five years later, Senator Chaney was dead. To his widow, he left everything he owned, including the ranch, with the Eyeglasses brand, near San Angelo.

"We don't see much of Mrs. Chaney between sessions of the legislature," the old-timer said. "She's usually here when they're sitting, lobbying for good schools and so on —and she don't just get up there and screech at them! This lady knows how to get things done."

"I imagine so," Hewitt said heartily. "Who is Dr. Lowell Chaney?"

"Brother of her husband, and he's sort of related to her some other way, too. Let's see, Lowell married a Cartwright, and Viola's mother was a Cartwright."

Hewitt was distraught and absent-minded all afternoon. There was not much he could have done, anyway, but his absorption in the problem that Mrs. Chaney represented made it a lost afternoon. But by evening, his mind was made up. It was not until seven-thirty that he went down to the dining room.

And there she was, in the corner that had always been his. She knew when he came into the room, but he stood and stared at her, smiling, with his head cocked to one side, until she looked up. Their eyes met. She bowed her head and spread her hands in a gesture of dismay.

She still wore that ghastly hat, but she was absolutely

enchanting despite it. He ignored the captain of waiters and crossed the room swiftly. She hardly waited for him to get there, to speak.

"I know, I know, I have your table."

"Well, an old, grouchy bachelor is entitled to his habits, ma'am."

"You're not that old, sir, and the least I can do is share the table with you. Will you settle for that?"

"If I may trade places with you, I should be delighted."

She stood up. "Another bachelor habit?"

They traded places. "Afraid so," he said with his warmest smile—and he could smile warmly, and knew it. "I'm alive today, ma'am, because I've made it a habit to sit with my back to the wall and my face to the door."

"Really! It sounds fascinating." She shuddered deliciously. "What are you, a soldier of fortune?"

"Just a private detective, ma'am."

"That sounds even more fascinating. I'm sure you'll want a whiskey before you eat, sir."

"No ma'am. I'll get some wine for us, if you'll share it, and if you know what's good."

"There usually isn't much choice. I trust Monty, the head waiter."

Well, he was making progress! At least he had learned who Monty was. He summoned the man, asked him to bring a bottle of good wine, and watched the fellow send a waiter off with his keys. The wine was served, and it was not bad. They were left alone at last, and now Mrs. Viola Dempsey Chaney had to get busy and earn her twelve dollars a day. He wondered how she would do it.

She closed her hands together under her chin and flashed her dimples at him in a smile. "I'm sure you know I planned this," she said demurely.

Oh, she was good! "I hoped so, Mrs. Chaney, but I can't imagine why."

"Oh . . . you're a man's man, the kind I learned to trust when I was a little girl. Your word would be good, you'd never be cruel or spiteful. A man who carries a gun in a shoulder holster, who can carry on an intelligent conversation—oh, I'm shameless, I should be letting you say nice things about me, shouldn't I?"

"I plan to, but first—how did you know about the shoulder holster? I know you didn't feel it when I helped you across the lobby. I saw to that."

"I look for them. My daddy wore one, and so did my husband."

"Who was a state senator of the reform bloc, a leader in the fight for decent schools, and a cattleman up around San Angelo."

Their eyes met, and she blushed slightly. "I do feel better," she said softly. "You asked around about me, didn't you? So you wanted to meet me, too!"

"Very much." He leaned across the table to pour her another glass of wine. "I almost took a case in San Angelo a few years back. A bank that was in trouble," he went on meretriciously. But safely, too; it was hard to find a city of any size in the west that had not had a bank in trouble of some kind in recent years.

"That would be Security United," she said angrily. "I wish you had been there! Or someone who could get the truth out of those people. The two investigators who were there just were no good at all! The president shot himself, and the cashier is still a fugitive, and they still can't reopen the bank because it's still tied up in court."

He encouraged her to talk about the Security United Bank troubles, in which she had lost more than two thousand dollars and still could lose another two thousand tied up in the courts. He fired questions at her rapidly.

"That first investigator—what was his name?"

"Mark O. Patterson, and he's still getting paid after four years! All those expenses have to come out of the depositors' money."

"The other one—is he still on the case?"

"He comes and goes. That's I. J. Phillips, who represented the underwriter that bonded the fugitive cashier. Anything to get out of paying!"

"I'm afraid that's part of the game, ma'am, for all too many private detectives. Where does old Johnny Quillen figure into it?"

"Oh, Johnny had nothing to do with that case. He's not even—"

She fell silent, a deathly sort of silence in which she turned deathly pale. He thought she was going to faint, when she realized how he had trapped her. He quickly poured her another glass of wine, and got up to go around the table to help her drink it. He put his hand on the back of her neck and put the glass to her lips, and she emptied the glass and shook off his hand. He returned to his side of the table and sat down.

She could not bear to look at him. She closed her eyes and said, "I sat here like a fool, like a *fool,* and just blabbed away."

"Not as much as you're going to blab, ma'am."

She opened her eyes, and they were glittering with anger. "You made a fool of me. That wasn't necessary. I would not expect you to be so cruel."

A waiter condescended to call. He ordered dinner for them, and waited until they were alone again.

"It's life that's cruel, ma'am, and there's only one winner

in most games. Very few people have fooled me as badly as you did at first."

"What did I do wrong?"

"My dear, as clumsy as I am, I could have marched a piper's band in kilts down those stairs without bumping into anyone. That's where you went wrong, faking a lame foot so early in the game. You had plenty of time to meet me, and if you're going to stay in this business—"

She cut in, "That's where you're wrong, Mr. Genius! I was just going to pass close enough to you to look you over—"

"And let me look you over—"

She smiled. "Well, yes, and then let *you* figure out how to make *my* acquaintance. But I do have a bad foot, and I did stumble into you."

"Ma'am, the bewildering thing about you is that you're too pretty, too smart, too good to be true. And yet I do believe you, and am honored to know you."

"Do you really mean that?"

"Yes. Shall we shake?"

"Oh, please!" Her hand came out to clasp his. "First names, too? People call me Vi."

"And I'm Jeff to a few friends. Too bad Johnny Quillen can't join us."

"I can get a message to him."

"Through Monty?"

Again her eyes blazed with anger. "Damn you, did you rattle my room? That's the only way you could have found that out!"

"Vi, you're not going to last in this business, if you have scruples about searching somebody's room."

"Then I shall have none. I can be good at this job, Jeff, I know I can! I've worked for the Mop before, and did a good job. But they're prejudiced against women in any job, and if Johnny could have thought of any other way to get on your blind side, I wouldn't have got this one. But I can be good at anything I set out to do, and I like investigative work, and I'm going to make them keep me on!"

"The one thing I can't figure out," he said, "is why all the new clothes? And why that hat?"

She laughed merrily. "Just no reason to buy clothes on a San Angelo cow ranch. Johnny said you were a fanatic about women's clothes, but that I should leave one thing for you to criticize and correct. He said that when you asked to buy me a hat, I would know I had won."

"He'll pay for it, but I'll pick it out. Whistle for Monty, my dear. Let's have Johnny join us."

He had Monty bring paper and an envelope. He had Mrs. Chaney address the envelope, so Johnny would open it unsuspectingly. But Hewitt wrote and signed the note inside:

Dear Johnny:
 Join us at dinner, and then tomorrow you can buy
Vi a hat, which I will select. Shame on you!

Jeff

CHAPTER FIVE

They sat so late at the table that only the waiters remained to watch them finish their last pot of coffee. "Same old Agate Eyes!" Johnny growled. "Well, I don't mean to be hornswoggled this time. I want to know how you got onto this case before I say a word."

"Johnny, I don't even know what you're working on," Hewitt said truthfully and for the tenth time. "I'm not even sure what I'm working on. I don't see how they fit together, your case and mine."

"Then you go your way, and I'll go mine."

"Suit yourself."

Johnny leaned back in his chair and glowered at him angrily. "If that's the way you want it, all right, but by God, it makes me mad when you tell me those childish lies and expect me to believe them!"

"I haven't told you a single lie."

"The hell you haven't! Or Conrad did."

"What did Conrad lie to you about?"

"He said you was on a bank fraud case, nothing more or less. Ha! I spend six months and two thousand dollars on the biggest case I ever handled. Just when I'm getting close to it, there you are, spang in my sights."

Hewitt looked at Vi Chaney. She had been watching and listening intently, her face flushed with excitement and prettier than ever, but in silence. Johnny had snubbed her coldly from the first. Hewitt knew that the woman was angry, and he admired her for the self-control that enabled her to listen and learn, instead of quarreling.

He looked back at Quillen. "My lad, I closed my fraud case. I can refer you to the banker who paid us. I can refer you to the sheriff who—"

"William W. Wetherly?" Johnny cut in. "That's what I mean, Agate Eyes. He double-crossed me, too. Everything he knows about the case, I told him. All right, the one thing I don't stand for is a double-cross! And I been double-crossed by everybody—Wetherly, and Vi, and you. And of course it's mostly you."

"Bill Wetherly never said a word about another case. If you want to know what I'm working on—"

Hewitt tossed the fifty-dollar slick on the table. Quillen picked it up, looked at both sides, and dropped it again. "Not much good. You looking for a counterfeiter? No profit in that."

Mrs. Chaney had picked up the coin and was studying it carefully. She looked up and caught Hewitt's eye. He said, "Fair enough, Johnny. I'll work the counterfeit case, and nothing else, I promise. You work your case and I won't butt in. Who gets Mrs. Chaney?"

"She ain't working for me," Johnny said, without looking at her. "She double-crossed me. You take her."

"Is it a deal?" Hewitt asked her.

"Not at any twelve dollars a day," she said demurely. "I come in as a partner, or not at all."

"Fair enough."

Quillen said, "Then you start out, Agate Eyes, by paying me back four hundred dollars expense money I advanced her. And she's already drawed one paycheck for nine days. That's a hundred and eight dollars."

Hewitt made as if to stand up. "Well, I'd say you have

a good lawsuit there, Johnny—if you can persuade the Missouri Pacific to file it. They may not be as anxious as you to admit they played the easy mark. I'll say good night to both of you. These are long, busy days for me."

Quillen looked at him almost piteously. "Sit down, you son of a gun."

"And be called a liar and double-crosser again?"

"I take it back."

Hewitt sat down. "Once more," he said, raising his right hand, "I take oath that I don't know what case you're working, and as far as I'm aware, neither does Conrad."

"There ain't no such coincidence this big, Agate Eyes, a million-dollar case that you just *happen* to blunder into the neighborhood. Things like that don't happen," Johnny said.

Hewitt felt a small inner twitch of something that was not quite excitement, but which was still stronger than mere interest. He believed in hunches devoutly, and had long ago learned not to court regret by ignoring them. The human mind, he felt sure, knew a lot more than it thought it did. It took in knowledge without registering it consciously, and responded with a "hunch" when something touched one of the sensitive spots that a man did not know were in his mind.

"I don't believe much in coincidence, either," he said, slowly. "You claim you're looking for a big one. I *know* I'm looking for one. What'll you bet they turn out to be the same man?"

"A counterfeiter? Give me that coin again!" Quillen snatched it from Vi's hand, and studied it again. "It ain't very good, Agate Eyes. You and I both know engravers that could do a better job. This is some amateur piece."

"We all start out as amateurs. You noticed, I hope, that there's a gold wash on it."

"Sure. A process called electroplating. The Germans are good at it. All right for jewelry that don't get much friction. But the way coins are handled, this will wear off in a matter of weeks."

"It will last long enough to fool someone who is not very expert on American coinage. Someone anxious to buy up to a million dollars' worth at half price. The greedier they are, Johnny, the easier they are for a grifter to set up, and those were machine-made. Even the milling is die-stamped. If this fellow has a power-driven die-stamp press, and can do his own plating, I figure he can probably turn out from one thousand to two thousand of them a day, by himself."

Quillen's big hand clenched so tightly around the coin that his knuckles became white. He sucked in his lower lip and whistled softly.

Then his hand relaxed, and let the coin fall on the table. He shook his head.

"No, it ain't the same case. You're talking about a machinist and diemaker, and I'm talking about a Russian nobleman, a son of a bitch who is a murderer and a thief who got away with a hundred and twenty thousand dollars in currency."

Hewitt frowned. "Why haven't I heard about a case as big as that?"

"Because I was told to drop everything else, and handle it personally."

"And you thought you could do it without splitting with your oldest friend in the business? Shame on you!"

"I've split with you before," Quillen said, his heavy face turning red, "and it's always the way the butcher made his sausage—half rabbit, and half horse meat. One rabbit to one horse."

"You were willing to cut Mrs. Chaney in on it," Hewitt

said sorrowfully. "You would give her the facts, but not me. You don't deserve any consideration, Johnny."

"I was told nothing," Vi Chaney said quickly. "I was merely told to find out what you knew about it."

"Then you're entitled to full wages," Hewitt told her, "because you found out exactly nothing, and exactly nothing is what I know about it."

"She's entitled to nothing," said Johnny. "She's the same as any other woman, where you're concerned. They all just swoon for you."

Hewitt and Vi smiled at each other, and then he turned back to Johnny. "Are we partners?"

"I reckon."

"Then start talking."

Johnny talked. He had made his usual methodical background investigation, and he still had the memory that was like some enormous and orderly warehouse. It stored literally thousands of facts, and Quillen could find the one he wanted instantly. . . .

Not quite a year ago, a messenger for the Great Coast Bank and Trust Company, in New York, had gone to the Eighth Street office of the Manhattan Conveyancing Company, a firm of land title experts, to pick up $120,000 on a property deal. Title had been searched, an abstract signed by a judge, and the deal closed, that day. It was a familiar procedure to all parties. The messenger certainly was familiar to the trust officer at the conveyancing company.

It was raining that day. The messenger wore yellow oilskins. Naturally, he did not remove them for the few brief moments it took for him to sign for the little satchel of hundred-dollar bills.

"Bad day to be out. You've had a wet walk. I hope this doesn't bring on your rheumatism, Chester," the trust officer said.

Chester Larrick, the old war veteran who was Great Coast's messenger, made a sound that was half squeak and half growl. He threw his head back and lifted his graying beard enough to show the trust officer the red flannel rag that was wrapped around his neck. Chester had been wounded, first at Ball's Bluff and again at Antietam, this time in the throat. His voice was unreliable to begin with, and with a cold, it left him entirely.

He walked out with the money in a canvas satchel, clumping along in his heavy rubber boots. He never showed up at the bank. It was naturally assumed that he had been killed for the money, somehow, in the block and a half between the two offices. Less than an hour after the alarm was given, two detectives went to his rooming house, hoping to turn up something that would lead them to his murderer.

Instead, they found his body, dead, the coroner's physician said, almost twelve hours. So it had not been Chester Larrick, but a very talented impostor, who had picked up the money at Manhattan Conveyancing Company. Even with the gloomy light and the noise of the rain on the skylight, it took acting ability that was close to genius to fool the officer into handing over the money, not merely without suspicion, but with a word of sympathy for Chester's rheumatism.

Since Chester had been a solitary man, it took time to unravel the case, time to determine that he had made at least one friend. This was a much younger man, who had introduced Chester to the mysteries of chess. They had

played a few times in Chester's room, but usually he went
to his new friend's quarters—wherever they were.

It took still more time to find an acquaintance of Chester's who had seen him with his new friend. The detectives
had luck, this time. This acquaintance had also seen Chester's new friend a night or two after seeing him and Chester
together. His story was almost incredible—at first.

Quillen said, "But they found quite a few people who
saw this fella that same night. It was at some kind of Slo-
venian dance, and he was having himself a great old time.
Pretty drunk, dancing with all the girls, bragging about his
family in the Old Country—and you can believe this or
not, Agate Eyes, but wearing a monocle, too! Claimed his
name was Kol Korzinsky, something like that, and he was
the nephew of the Count of Kossackthen and Sapoldi and
Sibinga. Naturally, there ain't no such count and no such
places.

"But at least they found out that he could talk Polish and
Russian and German, and dance like a fool. Nobody had
ever seen him around there before. They never seen him
around there again. I reckon the man we're after for killing
Chester Larrick and stealing that money is the one that ro-
manced all the girls at that dance, the night he got drunk.
Can you beat that, Agate Eyes? A monocle, and claimed
to be a count!"

Hewitt drummed on the table, staring blindly at Vi
Chaney's face. "The money," he said, "was all in one-
hundred dollar bills? They're not exactly easy to pass. They
have to be discounted, in those quantities."

"These were. They first turned up in London, not very
long ago. Scotland Yard knows who brought them from
New York, although they'll never prove it on him. He
couldn't have swung the deal for the whole hundred and

twenty thousand, but they figger he paid about five thousand in cash for say, ten thousand in hundreds. There's
still better than a hundred thousand missing."

"What's the reward?"

"Half of everything that can be recovered from the
money, plus ten thousand for finding and convicting the
murderer of Chester Larrick."

"Lot of money for an old bachelor war veteran."

"He was a bank's old bachelor war veteran. They can't
afford to let people get gay with their messengers."

"How well did this fake count speak English?"

"Spoke it well."

"With an accent?"

"Like any foreigner, they said, but he spoke better American than many a native, except for that accent."

"Would it sound like a British accent?"

"Well, from what I can find out—not if you knowed
many Britishers or Russians. If you did, it'd sound
Russian."

"Physical description, Johnny."

"Six feet two. Hundred and ninety pounds. Big shoulders
and hands. Fair hair, but going a little bald on top. Blue
eyes. Flat nose, big chin, straight mouth with small teeth.
The women went for him."

"How did he kill Larrick?"

"Knife. Knowed what he was doing, too. Larrick wasn't
drunk or drugged or anything like that. Been sitting in a
chair, and this fella slipped the blade between his ribs and
straight into his heart. Anybody that good didn't have to
cut his throat afterward, but he done it."

"Johnny, we're both looking for the same man."

"You sound pretty confident," Vi said. It was her first
comment.

"I am. The New York job was just to raise capital. If he moved those bills fast, he was dealing with someone who was waiting for them, and he didn't get more than thirty cents on the dollar."

"That's about the market price, but it still comes out thirty-six thousand dollars, Agate Eyes."

"The counterfeiting is still his big stroke, but it takes money to buy the kind of equipment he has. He needs cash that he can spend until he moves his slicks, too. No, thirty-six thousand would just about finance him."

"How does he move the gold?"

"Probably in Mexico, where they're not that familiar with American coins. He could take all kinds of currency and gold in return—American, British, French, German, Austrian. If he moves a million dollars' worth of slicks, he comes out of it with half a million in spendable money. Two million, and he's a real millionaire."

Johnny wrung his hands. "All right, how do we split up the deal?"

"Even. I've already got one case where we'll get a third of everything we recover, and it's ten thousand that's missing. I think we'll get most of it back. I'll throw that in. Say we make three thousand—that's a thousand each."

Johnny looked first at Hewitt and then at Mrs. Chaney. "Even split, but three ways? You must think I'm crazy! If you want Vi in on it, pay her out of your share."

"No. We need her."

"Why?"

"The bogus count is a ladies' man. She could be the shortest route to him."

Johnny shook his head. "This ain't a game for women, Agate Eyes."

Before Hewitt could answer, Vi said hotly, "If a man can do it, I can! I've listened to all of your brag I care to listen to, Johnny, and I will not be humiliated by you again —I *will not,* do you hear? Treated like a half-witted child just because I'm a woman, paid coolie wages instead of an operative's pay, and now you have the effrontery to tell me that this isn't a game for women!"

Johnny looked at Hewitt, who said, "You got yourself into this, my boy—let's see you get yourself out." Johnny ran his hands through his thinning, graying hair.

"Vi, it's dangerous. This man's a killer."

"I'll outshoot you with either a thirty-eight or a shotgun. Damn it, what do you think I do to pass the time on the ranch? I shoot. I'm not afraid of any man alive, and I've got a thirty-eight of my own."

"Now listen, Vi, I don't want to make you no madder than you are. I like you, and I respect women—you know that! It's because I respect you so much that I don't want to get you into no dirty situation like this. Why, this killer might be right here in Austin!"

Mrs. Chaney stood up. She did not look at Hewitt.

"I think he is," she said, picking up her handbag. "Very well, if I'm out, I'm out. So I shall just have to cash in on Count Kotrzina all by my poor, weak, feminine self!"

"Cash in on *who?*"

She smiled down at him. "The world explorer and lecturer, discoverer of the Popectasetl ruins in San Luis Potosí, former household adviser to the Raja of Fettebang, former professor of Greek literature at—"

"Count *who?*" Johnny almost shouted. He jumped up and grabbed her by the arm. "What are you talking about?"

"I loathe grabbers. Let go of me!" Johnny let go. She

smiled and nodded her thanks. "What was the name of your bogus count at the dance?"

"Kol Korzinsky or something like that, and he wasn't a count. Just the nephew of one."

"Now he's a full-fledged count, and his first name is Carl, not Kol, and his family name is spelled capital K, o, t, r, z, i, n, a. He's three times related to the Hohenzollerns and twice to the Battenbergs and twice to the Romanovs, and he and I had dinner in this very dining room the first night I was here. He is utterly charming!"

Hewitt said nothing. Johnny reached across the table to pluck a cigar from Hewitt's pocket. "Sit down, Vi. May I smoke?" he said.

"Certainly. Am I in?"

"You're in," said Johnny. He grimaced at Hewitt. "I guess I'm in a losing streak. Now you tell us what you know about our nobleman friend."

Hewitt told them about Doc Nolan, and the stranger with the British accent who had informed Sheriff Wetherly that Hewitt wore a .45 under his coat. He told them about his agreement with Simon Taylor. Johnny chuckled.

"I traced my party, through a railroad ticket, to that same part of Texas. I heard that Bill Wetherly was a pretty superior kind of a country sheriff, so I wired him to be on the lookout for him. Then what happens? Why, he talks to him and lets him get on the next train out of town!"

"Don't sell Bill Wetherly for less than market, Johnny. What were the names of those places the bogus count came from?"

"I wrote these down. They're as close as anybody could come, remembering it from the dance—Kossackthen and Sapoldi and Sibinga."

Hewitt looked at Vi, who shook her head. "He didn't talk much about his European background. Those are unfamiliar to me."

"My best information is that he headquarters here in Austin, or somewhere pretty close to it," said Johnny. "Any idea where he lives?"

"No," said Vi, with her sweetest smile, "but if you had only condescended to tell me what we're really looking for, instead of trying to make me seduce Mr. Hewitt, I might have found out. He was just a pleasant dinner companion to me, and when you're working for cheap pay, for cheapskates, it's always nice to have a personable gentleman buy your dinner."

"I didn't tell you to seduce Agate Eyes," said Johnny, "and if you fall for every knife murderer you meet, you ain't going to last long in this game. I told you, it's a man's game, Vi! I want Agate Eyes to walk home with me, so he'll know where to find me in a hurry. I don't go out on the street much. Good chance this fella already knows about me."

They stood up and left the hotel dining room together, to the enormous relief of the employees. As they walked, Vi between them, holding an arm of each, she lectured Johnny sternly:

"Women won't forever be docile to the arrogance of you men. Women can do anything, and soon they'll insist on having their chance to prove it. I'm just a little ahead of my time, is all. You might find yourself working for a woman chief of investigators, Johnny. And you'd find that everything was just as good as before, and probably better."

"Ha!" Quillen grunted.

They were passing the construction site of the new capitol building, which loomed up larger than life in the pale moonlight. There was a night watchman's fire burning in an open space, but the watchman was probably making his rounds, since he was not visible. They crossed a street and, in the darkness of shadow, felt their way along a wooden fence that had been erected around an excavation.

The shriek of the bullet, and its thud as it struck a heavy post in the fence, caused a reflex action in Hewitt that was faster than thought. He dropped, pulling Vi down with him and shouting, "Down, down," to Johnny. Quillen was only a fraction of a second slower.

The second bullet seemed to strike just as they heard the report from the first. It struck something harder than wood, and screamed louder. Johnny said, "Ah-h-h!" and went down on his knees and then fell forward on his face.

Hewitt saw a man on the flat roof of a building a block away. He got only a glimpse, not enough to know what he looked like, but enough to suggest that he had a rifle in his hand. He snatched the .38 out of his armpit and fired twice, just to let the fellow know he had been seen.

The man disappeared. The watchman came running through the littered capitol grounds, carrying a lantern. Johnny Quillen was muttering under his breath and trying to sit up. Vi had already sat up, and was looking around calmly. She pointed.

"There he goes," she said.

The man with the rifle was just walking swiftly around a corner. Hewitt said, "No use going after him now, and I don't think he'll try us again, anyway. Let's see how badly Johnny has been hurt, and where."

"Across the shoulder blade. A ricochet," Johnny said between his teeth. "How is my coat?"

The watchman arrived and held his lantern for Hewitt. "Ruined, and you're bleeding badly," Hewitt said.

"A brand-new suit. Wonder which one of us he was shooting at?" Johnny said coolly. "Help me up, Agate Eyes. This hurts like the very devil. Vi, go get the doctor and meet us at my place. We'll make it there all right."

Vi looked at Hewitt, who nodded. He saw her take her .38 out of her handbag as she began running. He and Johnny began walking. After a few steps, Johnny threw off Hewitt's supporting arm and walked along strongly. "My place is used by one of the big wheels in the legislature when it's in session," Johnny said. "Had to do a little dealing to get it, and I'm registered under the name of Sam Baum."

"Don't try to talk," said Hewitt.

Quillen went on talking. "He could've been firing at either one of us. What worries me, he's seen us both with Viola Chaney. She's a dead duck, if she smart-alecks around having dinner with him any more. I don't want to be responsible for anything happening to her. I knowed her husband and her father, Agate Eyes."

"We'll try to keep her whole," said Hewitt.

Johnny's room was a luxurious second-floor parlor with the bed in a curtained nook, and a dumb-waiter to bring up meals from the first floor. Dr. Lowell Chaney arrived with Vi before Hewitt had got Quillen's coat off. Hewitt liked the doctor immediately.

"Not a dangerous wound unless, of course, it gets infected. But it's going to take some needlework, and I'm going to have to give you a little chloroform."

"No you ain't," said Johnny. "Stitch away!"

He sat down astride a straight chair and leaned his chin on his good left arm on the back of it, while the doctor worked on his right shoulder blade. Hewitt ambled about

the room, examining the bookcases with particular care.
The books were almost all history and geography reference
books. He opened a big, flat atlas and carried it to where
there was a better light.

Vi came over and tried to see over his shoulder. "Looking for anything in particular?" she said.

"For place names in eastern Germany that sound like
Kossackthen, Sibinga, and Sapoldi."

"Try Poland, too."

Smart girl! He liked the way her mind worked, and he
liked it that she could be businesslike and direct without
being any less feminine.

It was almost daylight when they left Johnny's luxurious
quarters. The big railroad detective stood pain better than
anyone Hewitt had ever known. The doctor had told him
he would have to be quiet for a few days, but five minutes
after he was gone, Johnny was at his desk, writing letters.
Two stiff drinks were all the medicine he wanted.

"I think I'm going to have a bellboy go into my room,
before I go in myself, after this," Vi said, as they left the
house.

"I've got to send a telegram. If you feel like walking down
to the depot with me, I'll check your room out before you
go in," said Hewitt.

She did not answer, but merely tucked her hand into
his arm and hurried along beside him. The wire he sent
was to his partner, Conrad Meuse, a man whose odds and
ends of apparently unrelated knowledge always amazed
Hewitt. This would give him something to worry about:

MUST KNOW URGENTEST IF YOU CAN IDENTIFY
COUNT CARL KOTRZINA OR KORZINSKY OF APOLDA
AND CYBINKA AND OTHER PLACE SOUNDS LIKE

KOSSACKTHEN STOP IS HE WANTED BY ANYONE
FOR ANYTHING STOP IS FAMILY RICH STOP IS
INSANITY IN FAMILY STOP ANYTHING ELSE YOU
BELIEVE INDICATES POTENTIAL FOR COMPLEX
CRIME.

Vi touched the word, "insanity," and shivered. "I'm glad
you put that in. He's the most egotistical man I have ever
known in my life. He went out of his way to be charming
to me, but I'd hate to be his enemy."

"I'm afraid you are one now. Let's go back to the Condon House and check out your room."

Again she took his arm. "Do you think it was he who
shot Johnny?"

"Almost without question."

"Which one of you was he shooting at?"

"It might have been both of us. It probably was, and
what shook him up was seeing the girl of his dreams between us. That might disrupt the aim of an egotist of the
kind you describe, Vi. Next time, he might try for you first."

They reached the hotel and decided against an early
breakfast. The night clerk was dozing at the desk, and he
did not awaken as they went softly up the stairs. They
passed Hewitt's room and went on down the dark hall to
hers. She handed him her key, and stood aside while he
opened the door.

"Better leave a lamp burning, after this," he whispered.

He went in, crossed the room, and raised the blinds.
He opened both closets, and the bathroom, and even looked
under the bed.

Vi came in. He gave her the key. "Be sure it's locked
and bolted. Let's take no chances," he said.

"Don't worry, I shall! Thank you, Jeff, and if it isn't too
late in the day—good night."

She put her hand on his chest and tilted back her head. He kissed her lightly on the lips and went out. He heard the lock turn, the bolt being shot, before he went to his own room and a morning of light, uneasy sleep.

CHAPTER SIX

When he went to breakfast, late the next morning, three well-dressed men were sitting at the table that was, by long and honorable custom, his own. The seat with its back to the wall, however, was empty. He crossed the dining room with a scowl, noticing that the waiters were conspicuously absent.

One of the men at the table nodded to him, but did not get up. He was a little older than Hewitt, and considerably heavier. He wore a short, brown beard and, since Hewitt had last seen him, a pair of glasses attached to a black silk ribbon.

"Sit down, Jefferson. You notice that we waited breakfast on you, like one hog waits on another," he said.

"I notice. And of course these are Secret Service men, Denny, and it's only a pleasant social call," Hewitt said, sitting down.

"Of course. Jeff, meet Hugh Pikus and Milton Asbury. What's this ridiculous theory about a big gold-counterfeiting operation?" said Denny McGucken, former policeman, and now an attorney for the United States Treasury.

A waiter came. Hewitt ordered ham and three eggs, and waited until the coffee had arrived. When the waiter had turned his back, Hewitt dropped the slick fifty-dollar piece on the table in front of Denny.

"How's that for a ridiculous theory? Excuse me, there's a lady I know. I want her to eat with us," said Hewitt.

He stood up and smiled at Vi Chaney. Denny quickly hid the coin in his palm. "Why?" he said. "If you want to talk business, let's do so, and you feed your lady friend later."

"You're going to pay for her meal as well as mine," said Hewitt, "and she's my partner in this operation. If it's not fit for her ears, it's not fit for mine. Make room, somebody."

They made room. One of the Secret Service men brought a chair from another table, seating Vi between Denny and Hewitt. Again there was a wait, while Vi ordered. Hewitt liked her for ordering a hearty meal of ham and eggs. He distrusted women who fiddled stylishly with their food to make an impression, and then gorged secretly on chocolates and cake.

"What do you think of that minting job, Denny?" Hewitt said after the introductions had been completed.

Denny reluctantly exposed the coin. He examined it carefully and handed it to one of the Secret Service men. "Brass, with a gold wash," he said. "Indifferent engraving and the wrong date. The government never minted many fifties, you know."

"No, I didn't, but it's a nice thing to know in my business."

"The counterfeiter of that didn't know it either, that's obvious."

"Or didn't care, Denny. If he's allowed to go into full competition with the government, on his own terms, the credit of the United States could collapse so suddenly that he could probably buy the whole country at bankrupt sale. Yes, and pay for it with these slicks!"

Denny winced. "It would be hard to affect the credit of the nation by faking coins that were never minted."

Hewitt said nothing. He drank coffee and smiled at Vi, who smiled back. "I had a message from our mutual friend, Jeff," she said. "He slept badly and is in a ferocious mood this morning. He agrees now that he'll be room-bound longer than he thought last night."

"Good for his soul," said Hewitt.

The waiters arrived with their orders of ham and eggs. Denny fidgeted and glowered. The two Secret Service men passed the coin back and forth between them.

"No one can get very far by minting fifties. The whole world knows how few of them there are!" Denny burst out.

Hewitt nodded and smiled at him. "That's a great comfort to me, Denny. The way I had it figured, we're either going to buy up millions of dollars of those same coins at face value, or have our credit cut off here and there. It would be something new in big-scale crime, I grant you. It has never been done before—putting millions of dollars into circulation, in a distinctive new design, and let the United States try to explain. But that doesn't mean that it can't be done, Denny. Or so I thought, until I had your expert advice."

Denny said, pleadingly, "Jefferson, what's the story here? Naturally, any kind of counterfeiting is serious. Counterfeiting gold—well, I never heard of it before. Now and then, some carnival artist whittles out a lead coin or two, coats it with gold or brass, and passes it off on some country sucker. But the first time it hits a bank, even a country bank, it goes out of circulation bang-oh!"

"Denny, you used to be a copper. What do you read from that coin? I can tell you a little more about it, but you should be able to read the grim truth from that."

"It was struck by a steel die, I'd say, for one thing," said Pikus, the Secret Service man. "Engraving, I'd judge, rates from fair to poor."

"But it wasn't minted," said Hewitt, "by some clodhopper banging away with a sledge hammer. That was made by a machine. I've seen a collection of two thousand of them, and they all look exactly alike. And if you want my opinion, Denny, that was just about a short day's work for this son of a gun."

"That is not hard to believe. All right, let's concede, for the sake of argument, that our man can strike fifty thousand dollars a day in these coins. But then what does he do with them? This is where your theory falls down, it seems to me. Even good money is no good, if you can't spend it."

"The fifty thousand that I saw were sold for twenty cents on the dollar. That's a tempting discount—but it still leaves our man grossing ten thousand dollars for one day's work. I'll bet I could go down into Mexico, and within six months locate five million dollars in hoarded gold coin—American, British, German, French, Russian, Austrian. At twenty cents on the dollar, that would cost twenty-five millions of dollars in these defective beauties.

"Denny, if you're organized the way I think this fellow is organized, you could close out a campaign like that in three months, and be on your way with some of the heaviest luggage ever shipped out of Mexico. I may even be underrating him. Maybe he knows how to get to people who have hoarded up ten million—twenty million—thirty.

"The point is, when all this brass turns up, as it comes into circulation, there are going to be a lot of people just madder than hell at the United States of America. I'll make you another little bet right now, Denny. I'll bet that this isn't the first you have heard of these coins. Come clean with me! You wouldn't have come all the way out here to see me, if Uncle Sam wasn't already scared out of his pants."

Denny said stiffly, "I see I have to take you into my confidence, and I hope I can trust Mrs. Chaney."

"As far as you can me," said Hewitt.

"Somehow," said Denny, "I don't take much comfort from that assurance. I'll tell you all I know, though. The department had a report that one such coin had come into a bank in New Orleans. A Secret Service man, Adam Rhiner, was despatched there to look into it. He took possession of it, and wrote a rather detailed report on it, which he put in the mail."

"And then," said Hewitt, "he was murdered, and the coin disappeared."

Denny clenched his fist, but did not bring it down on the table. "By God, if you knew about that, and didn't let me in on it—!"

"I didn't. I'm only guessing. But I'll bet it was a knife murder, wasn't it?"

Denny looked at the two Secret Service men, muttering, "I told you, this fellow would make your hair stand on end. Milt, you saw Rhiner's body. Tell him about it."

Hewitt said quickly, "Not necessary. He was slashed to ribbons, wasn't he?"

Asbury nodded. "I've seen people cut up by savages in the cannibal islands in the East Indies. No worse than poor Adam Rhiner. We've kept it quiet that he was with the Service. But I'll tell you this, Mr. Hewitt—if you can help us lay hands on the vicious brute that did it, you'll make a friend of every Secret Service man in the Treasury."

"Nice," said Hewitt, "but not enough. We're talking about the most dangerous counterfeiter in history, as well as the killer of a Secret Service agent. I have two very good detectives who are my partners. How much reward will the Treasury pay?"

He looked at Denny, who ran his hands through his graying hair. "I believe I can go to five thousand," he said.

Hewitt's hand shot across the table to snatch up the slick coin. "Give me back my keepsake. I'm afraid we're going to have to work this case our own way."

"Jefferson, you can't let a man counterfeit the coinage of your own country and profit by it! If you do, I'll see that you go to the pen myself."

"Like to make me a little bet on that? You don't think I'm going to throw in with the counterfeiter, do you?"

"How else will you make money on it?"

"Let him peddle a million dollars in fake coins. Follow him around, make a deal to get the suckers' money back for them for a percentage of it. When we've cleaned up the case, chain Mr. Counterfeiter up and turn him over to the nearest sheriff."

"And make the Secret Service look like a bunch of music-hall comedians!" said Hugh Pikus.

Hewitt did not answer. He looked at Vi and said, "I wonder where they get their ham, here? I'd like to take a couple of hams back to Cheyenne with me, when we've finished this job."

"A sort of cousin of mine," she replied, smiling sweetly. "He raises his own hogs, does his own butchering, and smokes his ham and bacon according to a secret family recipe. It is good, isn't it?"

This time, Denny did bring his fist down on the table, so hard that coffee jumped out of the cup that the waiter had just refilled for Hewitt. "How much?" he choked. "How much does it take to get you to do the patriotic duty you ought to do anyway?"

"I'll have to consult my other partner."

"Who is your other partner?"

"Railroad detective by the name of Johnny Quillen. You may not know him, but—"

"Oh God! I know him. He has even less conscience than you, when it comes to money. How much, damn it?"

"For catching the murderer of your agent, and the counterfeiter, for catching him in the act of counterfeiting, moreover, so there is no doubt about a conviction, and for laying your official hands on his equipment, stock and coins in whatever stage of manufacture—thirty thousand dollars."

McGucken moaned. "The Secretary will never stand for it, Jefferson. It would break all precedent."

"I suggest that you spend the next several hours composing a long, explanatory telegram emphasizing the aspects of the national credit. Give him twenty-four hours to think it over."

"I'll see what I can do. Will you be here tomorrow at this time?"

"I very much doubt it, Denny."

"Then how am I going to let you know what the Secretary's answer is?"

Hewitt stood up, nodding and smiling to Vi, who stood up too. "You can let Mrs. Chaney know," he said. "I'm just going to assume that the Secretary agrees, because I'm quite sure he will. Better stay in Austin yourselves. One of us—Mrs. Chaney, or Johnny Quillen, or myself—will be in touch with you when we have any news. Good morning, gentlemen."

They left the dining room and went out into the street. Vi put on a good show, holding Hewitt's arm and looking up at him adoringly. Half a block down the street, she looked back and made sure that none of the Treasury men had followed them.

"Oh, cruel, cruel!" she whispered. "Oh, how could you

do it to them? Not the price, I mean, but just walking out without waiting to see if the Secretary accepts it. Oh, what wicked, cruel arrogance!"

"I'm not cruel, my dear. It's life that's cruel. Look, they're going to agree within twenty-four hours, aren't they?"

"I'm sure of it."

"Do it mercifully, and it will take a week for the Secretary to face the truth and come to an agreement. And in the long run, they'll all suffer more for having to give in. It's an axiom of life that the longer a decision is postponed, the more agonizing it is."

She thought that over. "Perhaps, but I still think there's a cruel streak in you. Where do you expect to be tomorrow morning?"

"I haven't the slightest idea. I just don't think Count Kotrzina is going to be found in Austin—not after missing two shots last night. Vi, how am I going to pick up his trail?"

She almost skipped like a little girl. "Oh, now I am really happy! Is the peerless detective, Jefferson Hewitt, really asking *me* for advice?"

"He sure is. I don't often admit I'm at a loss."

"Only when it pays, I'm sure." She became grave. "I don't know if I can help you, Jeff. He talked a lot, the kind of brag that doesn't really sound like brag, because he looks the part. But it was all generalities."

"Think, girl, think!"

"I have thought, believe me! There's a private banker in Matamoros, Mexico, an Englishman who—"

"Lawrence Makenroy?"

"Do you know him?"

"A little."

"What don't you know?" she said dispiritedly.

"What amazes me is how you know him. He runs what looks like a very modest business, but he represents an enormously wealthy British banking syndicate."

"He was my father's guest several times, and he visited my husband and me at the ranch, twice, to hunt prairie chickens. I am not exactly a barefoot farm girl."

"Well, not exactly," he agreed. "Now, where does Lawrence Makenroy come into this case?"

"He gives away little wax matches and big Cuban cigars, both with the firm's name on them. After dinner the other night, Carl brought out one of those cigars and lighted it with one of those matches."

"So he's already 'Carl' to you?"

"Yes, and I was 'Viola' to him. Not Vi, but Viola. He was so gallant, and so objectionably smooth about it! He has what my father used to call a vanity that is permanently chiseled into the marble of his brain."

He slipped an arm around her long enough to squeeze her upper arm. "You have what is required to make a go of this business, Vi. Sharp eyes. A quick, retentive memory. Excellent judgment of people. And perhaps most important of all, acting talent of high degree, to persuade people that you are not what you really are."

"I appreciate your saying that. I hope it's true."

"It's true, all right. I'm a good judge of character myself, and I never did think I was doing you a favor by making Johnny accept you as an equal partner. You'll earn your way."

"That's very important to me. I don't want favors just because I'm a pretty woman, Jeff."

"You won't get them, because I don't think you're very pretty at all."

That stopped her dead in her tracks. She stared at him a moment, eyes narrowing, cheeks turning pinkly angry.

She caught herself in time, and swung a small fist lightly at his stomach. "Damn you, Hewitt, and double-damn you!" she said and burst out laughing. "Where are we headed?"

"To bait the bear in his den."

"Johnny? Monty says he's in a terrible humor."

He was. His wound was at the most painful stage, and he still stubbornly refused to take a painkiller for it. He was stripped to the waist, unshaven, and bleary-eyed. He had found that the only comfortable position was the one in which his wound had been stitched—astride a straight chair, his right arm resting across it, so that there was a minimum of strain on the stitches.

"I even sleep this way," he said. "Worst of it is, Agate Eyes, maybe the son of a bitch was shooting at you! If I ever find out I'm treating you on this deal, I'll tie you naked to a cactus and feed you your own eyeballs."

Hewitt had considerable affection for the big man. This was no time to bait him. He pulled a chair up for Vi, and then sat down on the edge of the bed.

"But we're getting somewhere, Johnny, and each of us can keep busy for a few days without crossing one another's trails," he said.

"What can I do, laid up this way?"

"I'll come to that. First, let me tell you what Vi and I pulled off this morning. Denny McGucken is in town. We had breakfast with them."

"Them?"

"Denny and two Secret Service men who are with him. I'll tell you what we have worked out so far."

"No, let me," said Vi. "I sat there and watched it happen, Johnny. It was news to me, most of it, as it was to them. We're into something a lot bigger than we thought."

She told it well. Hewitt could see the look come into Johnny's eyes that meant he was forgetting his pain in his greed to earn and collect his share of a thirty-thousand reward. "What they don't realize," Vi said, "is that Jeff could probably round up the count in a few days, if he really tried. But no, to catch him in the act, we have to wait until he has turned out enough coin to make thirty thousand sound reasonable indeed!"

"Only we won't wait that long," Hewitt said. "Once the Secretary agrees to thirty thousand—or to any figure close to it—we'll make our move as soon as possible. I don't want any chance of this stuff getting into circulation."

"So you're going to Matamoros?"

"Yes."

"You don't think this Britisher is in on it?"

"No chance of that, Johnny. But he'll figure out some way to use Makenroy's files, or Makenroy's business associates, or something, in locating rich Mexicans who have hoarded gold coin away."

"You ought to wire Makenroy."

"I thought of that, but I don't know him that well. In fact, he looks at me with a rather fishy eye. If the count is there, and my wire reaches him while they're fraternizing in business or socially, it'll be the word of an absent gumshoe against a fellow aristocrat. Makenroy's older brother is the earl of something. Makenroy himself is entitled to call himself by a title, but he doesn't. Says he has only contempt for it, but I notice he never misses a chance to tell you about it. No, I've got to see him personally, no other way out."

"What about Vi?"

"She'll receive my mail and telegrams, and keep an eye out for the count himself. But no more dinner dates! If he knows enough about you and me to shoot at us, it's not safe for her to fool around there any more."

Vi cut in, "I'm not so sure. He doesn't credit me with

much intelligence. He assumed I was just an ignorant Texas ranch girl, and I was as silly as I could be."

"All the same, don't take chances! If you see or hear anything about him, get in touch with Johnny immediately. And if you ever feel unsafe in that hotel, don't hesitate to move in here where Johnny can keep an eye on you."

"Dunno what I could do, me a one-armed man," Johnny mourned. "I don't see how I can do anything, camped here like a gutshot butchering hog."

"You can surely command some help out of the Missouri Pacific."

"That I can, but help for what?"

"Wherever he's making the coins, I think he's buying finished brass stock in polished rods, and sawing out his own blanks. It would be too dangerous for him to buy blanks already cut in the dimensions of coins. It would take us forever to track down all the brass foundries that can turn out polished brass rod stock. But his minting works are here in Texas somewhere. How close can you come to tracking down any such shipments by rail?"

"I can sure try."

"They'll come wrapped, of course, and probably crated. They won't be labeled as brass milling stock, either. We don't know how long they'll be, but I'd say it would be hard for him to handle anything longer than four feet."

Johnny waved his big chin irritably. "I'll have them rattle all their files until we come up with something. As a guess, how big a shipment do you think it would be?"

"This," said Hewitt, "is where a guess is the best any of us can do. I don't know why he isn't turning out coins by the bushel right now. I'd say he has finished the spadework for selling them, because to the kind of orderly mind that can plan this job, that has to come first. The only reason I can think of for *not* being in production now is lack of brass stock."

Johnny nodded. "Has to be. Only bought enough to test his process, to begin with. Be crazy if he invested any more money in it, especially if he don't want it seen. How are you going to hide a quarter of a ton of brass rods? So what we're looking for, say, is a shipment of a couple of rods of brass about forty inches long. Say, seventy-five pounds, in a crate about three feet to four long, and in the neighborhood of six inches square the other way."

Hewitt got up to go. "I'll get back as soon as I can, but this Matamoros business could be important. Vi put us on this track, by the way."

Johnny nodded. "She's a good detective—for a woman."

"I ought to give you a friendly slap on the back for that," said Vi.

They returned to the hotel, where a telegram awaited Hewitt. It was from Conrad Meuse, and it said:

CARL ERIC HELMUTH VIKTOR OTTO KOTRZINA NOW HEIR TO TITLE COUNT OF KOTHEN COMMA OF APOLDA COMMA AND OF CYBINKA STOP FAMILY UNABLE LOCATE HIM STOP REWARD GOLD MARKS EQUAL FOUR THOUSAND PLUS DOLLARS STOP PRESENT COUNT AGED ILL STOP LAST OTHER HEIR DIED YEAR AGO STOP THIS IN OUR FILES FROM SAXONY FOR YEAR STOP WE SHOULD BE MOST GRATEFUL ASSIST NOBLE HEIR CLAIM WHAT COMING TO HIM STOP WHAT SHALL I DO MEANTIME

Hewitt leaned on the hotel desk to write out a brief answer, NOTHING. He handed Conrad's wire to Vi. "My goodness, yes, we shall all be most grateful to help him get what's coming to him," she said.

He liked her more and more. "I think you're a snob," he said. "Come help a miserable commoner pack."

CHAPTER SEVEN

He stepped off the train in a sweltering dusk, on a depot platform that was almost empty. An old, humped man standing beside a decrepit buggy, pulled by an ancient horse that was all bones, came hurrying toward him.

"Hidy, Mr. Hewitt, nice to see you again. Take you back to Miz Frank's place?"

Hewitt had not been in Brownsville for six years, but he seemed to remember old man, old hack and old horse. They seemed no older, no more decrepit. He wondered briefly if the old fellow was being paid to watch for him. No, Kotrzina was not that smart, not that attentive to detail.

"Is her bread just as good? Does she still make the same powerful coffee?" he said, smiling and handing the old man his suitcase.

"Yessir! She often mentions you, Mr. Hewitt. Just the other day, she says to me, she says 'Sol, you don't meet many true gentlemen in a town like this, do you? And I bet you know who I'm thinkin' about,' she says, and I did."

They got into the buggy together. Eventually the old horse got into motion. Sol Treegard, that was his name, and Hewitt had bought him a couple of drinks to celebrate his seventy-second birthday, six years ago!

Hewitt found one of his ever-ready five-dollar gold pieces in his watch pocket, and slipped it into Sol's hand. "I don't want anybody to recognize me, if I can help it, Sol," he said. "Mrs. Frank still have that little grove of trees beside her lane?"

"Yes, sir, she wouldn't cut them trees."

"All right, when we get there, we're going to wait in the grove, until we're sure there is no one else at her place. Then I want you to walk on ahead, and see her quietly and privately. You got that?"

"Yessir."

"If she has no other boarders, I'll stay there. If she has a boarder, I want to know what he looks like, and I don't want him to know I'm there until I know. Maybe she'll slip down the lane to see me, if she's alone, if you give her this."

He handed Sol another five-dollar piece. The horse took them creepingly around what Hewitt thought was one of the toughest, and at the same time, the most interesting, towns in the United States. Just across the Rio Grande, which emptied into the Gulf of Mexico only a few swampy miles away, lay another teeming, tough, and interesting city—Matamoros, in the Mexican state of Tamaulipas.

Together, Brownsville and Tamaulipas reminded Hewitt of cities like Singapore, Port Said, and Alexandria, all of which he had visited on cases. If you knew your way around, you could hire someone to kill a man for fifty dollars. If you did not, you could be the one killed for fifty. Both cities were policed as much by troops as by civil police. President Porfirio Diaz always kept one crack outfit of Mexican cavalrymen stationed in or near Matamoros; and on this side of the river, the U.S. horse soldiers were never far away.

They turned down a sandy lane, followed by the cloud of mosquitoes that were always Brownsville's first gift of welcome to the newcomer. It was an unprepossessing entrance, yet Hewitt's memory was of a pleasant old widow

whose boarding and rooming house actually was home-
like. A man hated to think of living in an isolated shanty
like this; and after he had been there a while, he hated to
leave it.

The horse did not have to be persuaded to stop under
the trees. Sol got down and, without a word, hobbled on
down the lane out of sight. It was pitch dark by now. Hewitt
sat there uneasily a moment, before lighting a cigar to repel
the mosquitoes. The glow of a cigar made a man a conspicuous target, but on the other hand, one did not like to
be eaten up by mosquitoes.

In a moment, he made out two figures approaching—
the tall, hunched Sol Treegard, and Mrs. Lettie Frank. The
woman came toward him with both hands outstretched,
and she lifted the billowing veil she wore against the
mosquitoes, to be kissed on the cheek. He thought, in the
dark, that her hair was a little whiter, but she had lost none
of her vigor.

"How are you, Aunt Lettie?" he said. "You're still wearing that enchanting perfume, so you haven't given up hope
of enslaving some man, that's sure."

She chuckled heartily. "How nice to talk to someone who
can joke again, Mr. Hewitt! People are so serious and dull,
nowadays. And what a thrill to keep a tryst with you in
the grove!"

"We'll get rid of Sol for a couple of hours, and scandalize
everybody."

She had to lift the veil again, to wipe her eyes. "I had
forgotten that people could say such outrageous things
with such an air. I don't understand the secrecy, Mr.
Hewitt. I have only one boarder now, a foreign gentleman,
most polite and reserved, and I'm sure most discreet. Whatever you're doing, I'm sure he wouldn't make any diffi-
culties."

"Let me describe him for you, Aunt Lettie. About forty, blue eyes, fair hair, tall and athletic-looking, and brilliant of mind and aristocratic of bearing."

"That describes Mr. Andreas perfectly. This is the third time he has stayed with me. He says he won't be here more than a day or two this time."

He took her by the arms. "Aunt Lettie, we're going to move him out tonight. This is one of the worst men in the world, believe me. You think of some excuse. I'll see to it that you get a telegram that a lot of relatives are coming, or something. Tell him he has to vacate, and I'll hide out here somewhere to make sure he does."

"Oh, I couldn't do that, Mr. Hewitt. Why, he has been the perfect guest! Most delightful, so charming—"

"So cold-blooded. Damn it, we can't argue about it. Do you think I'm a fool, Aunt Lettie?"

No, she certainly did not think him a fool, but neither could she force herself to tell Viktor Andreas that he must leave. "If he's only going to be here a day or two, why be so impetuous? I can't believe he would harm me, Mr. Hewitt. Why, he's hardly here at all! He rents a horse at the livery stable and only comes here to sleep," she said.

Well, he had learned one thing—that the count was now mounted. There was no moving her. Neither would she let him search Kotrzina's room.

They got back into the buggy. "I'll find another place to stay, but I'll get someone to come out and keep an eye on you, Aunt Lettie. Is there some work around the place that needs doing—some painting or mending of some kind?"

"Oh, I can't afford anything like that!"

"Well, I can. Remember those expense accounts of mine that shocked you so much? What'll it be?"

"Well, I have wanted the outside of the house painted for so long, but—"

"What color?"

"It has always been yellow."

"There'll be a man out here with yellow paint in the morning. Can you keep your head, now, and forget that I've been here at all? If you insist on keeping this man in your house, at least I've got to be assured that you're not going to make him suspicious of you."

"He will not be suspicious of me, Mr. Hewitt. I'm not going to ask you what Mr. Andreas has done. My lord, I guess I'm a gullible old fool! But I hope I have dignity enough to preserve my poise and peace of mind."

He raised the veil to kiss her wrinkled old cheek again. "You have, my dear. One thing more I want you to do."

"Oh dear, what now?"

"Fatten up a couple of these mosquitoes for me. I want to take them back home to roast."

On the way back to town, he questioned Sol Treegard. There was a different chief of police now. A new man ran the livery stable. No one that Hewitt remembered from previous visits seemed to be here now.

"If you want somebody to paint the house and protect Mrs. Frank, I can get you somebody. He's been in the pen, but he's reformed," said Sol.

"Who is he? What's his name?"

"Only name I know him by is Buzz Barron. But I tell you this, Mr. Hewitt, if that Mr. Andreas is a crook, Buzz will see through him. Ain't nobody going to fool him."

"Let's go see Mr. Barron."

Sol chuckled. "Hee-hee-hee! Ain't nobody called him 'mister' for so long, he won't know how to answer. But Buzz is your man."

"Just see that we aren't conspicuous, hunting and finding him, and you keep all this to yourself, too."

"Don't worry, Mr. Hewitt. I know who my friends is.

Nobody pays no attention to old Sol no more, either. I tell you, I'll take you to a family I know. Their kids is all married and moved away, and they'll have a room for you. I'll bring Buzz there."

They went to a modest little Mexican-style place, built around an unpaved central patio, and Hewitt rented a room that had its own private entrance. He could even rent a horse from the same man. There were no screens on the windows, but there was mosquito netting on a frame around his bed.

He lighted another cigar and sat in his dark little room until he heard Sol and another man in the patio. He opened the door and asked them in. Buzz Barron was a man of average height who seemed to walk in a sort of crouch. Hewitt could not decide whether he was a predatory animal or was merely on perpetual guard against predators.

"Buzz, this is Mr. Hewitt, that I told you about," said Sol in a low voice.

Barron said nothing. Hewitt put out his hand and said, "Nice to know you, Mr. Barron. Understand you did some big time. Mind telling me what for?"

Barron's handshake was exceedingly brief. He bit off his words as though he could not spare many. "Murder. I killed my wife," he said.

"Hard lines. What we want now is to keep Mrs. Frank alive, and Sol says you're the man for that. He also tells me that you're not going to be fooled by a smooth-talking, aristocratic killer. I'll tell you what this boarder of hers looks like, and I'd like to talk to you after you've seen him."

"Mr. Hewitt, what does this job pay?"

"Well . . . how about ten dollars a day, with a guarantee of a week?"

Hewitt had a feeling that a fist in the stomach would not have rocked Barron, but those figures did. "This job is on the up-and-up? This ain't no crook deal?" he said, when he had recovered his breath.

"Well, what do you think? I'm a suspicious man, too, Mr. Barron. But I've got to trust somebody. I don't know you from Adam, but I do know Sol Treegard, and I trust his judgment. All you have to do is paint that damned house and never let her out of your sight!"

"Where am I going to get paint and brushes and so forth? I know where I can get a ladder."

Hewitt handed over a gold double eagle. "Here's twenty dollars. Don't bring me back any change. We'll settle up when the job is over. If you want to draw ahead on your pay—"

"No, I don't. I'll be out there at daylight tomorrow. Have to arrange some way to meet you tomorrow night. If this boarder is like you say, I won't leave the place. Now what does he look like?"

Hewitt did not leave his rooming house the next day. Sol brought him a Mexican boy who could do one job for him. Benito was small, and looked no more than eleven or twelve. He was eighteen, intelligent, and adventurous. Hewitt put him to watching the border bridge for Kotrzina.

That evening, Sol brought him word that Barron had said that the boarder had not returned to Mrs. Frank's place. Neither had Benito seen him at the bridge. Hewitt sent Benito out to bring him another dozen cigars, and possessed himself in patience. The food was passable here, and between the cigars and the netting over his bed, he stood a good chance to survive the mosquitoes.

He was far from sure what he hoped to learn here, and he wished heartily that he had seen Kotrzina himself, and had made his own appraisal of the man. Vi was both a good judge and a good reporter. He could trust her estimate further than he could that of most people, but there was nothing like his own judgment.

From what he had seen so far, he had built up a picture of a man who could plan imaginatively, boldly, and with the attention to detail that big plans required. He was an unscrupulous, unfeeling, egotistical loner, a man of secrets, a man who lived among the dreams and appetites in his own foul mind. Most of the time, he wanted no one close to him, needed no one.

Yet now and then he had to strut, too, as when he had taken Vi to dinner and bragged about his noble blood. He could make mistakes, too, and exterminate them (he hoped!) by exterminating people as he had Doc Nolan. He could slink like a vicious old tomcat most of the time, yet surely he had the social background to be the genial lordship among real lordships.

And one thing was sure, he had a temper that at times went out of control. One time was when he had slashed Doc Nolan to death. Another time was when he had shot at them in the dark—an impossible rifle shot by any measurement—without caring if he hit a woman. Or perhaps it had been the woman he was trying to kill or wound or warn off.

Kotrzina had not come to Brownsville simply in a flight of panic, after merely wounding Johnny Quillen. He might have changed his timing a little because of that, but the alert Vi had definitely tied this area into Kotrzina's operational plans. When she recognized Lawrence Makenroy's cigar and matches, she punched a big hole in the count's defenses.

Hewitt was still asleep, on the second morning in Brownsville, when Benito slipped into his room and closed the door. Hewitt rolled over and had the .38 out from under his pillow before the boy could close the door. Benito grinned at him.

"I ain't going to come in here this way at night, believe me!" he said.

"If you do," said Hewitt, grinning and rolling out of bed, "better give the password first. What time is it, and what's doing?"

"Seven-thirty, somewhere like that, and the man you told me about came back from Matamoros this morning."

Hewitt's pulse jumped. "You're sure it's him?"

"Sure I'm sure! You said he hired a horse at the city stables, didn't you? I went over and asked what horse they rented out to a big tall foreigner, and it was Buster. I know all their horses, Mr. Hewitt."

"And this man was riding Buster."

"That's what I'm trying to tell you."

"What shape was he in, and what shape was Buster in?"

"Oh, you know how to figger that, too, do you?" The boy grinned. "This man, he's about to sleep in the saddle—you know? He had a long, hard night. But Buster, he's full of life, see? He's been tied somewhere all night, while the man is tying on a load."

Hewitt smiled, stepped into his pants, and began stropping his razor. "That's how you tell, is it?"

"Yes. The man, he went down the road to Mrs. Frank's house. I think he'll sleep all day."

"That earns you a bonus, Benito. Now you go home and sleep all day, too. We're sure it's the right man, are we?"

"Looks like him, and it's the right horse, Mr. Hewitt. So it has to be the right man."

"Benito, keep this up and someday, you're going to be a detective."

He sent the boy to his landlady to ask for a hurried breakfast. He saddled the horse he had rented from her husband while it was being prepared, and thirty minutes later was crossing the bridge into Mexico.

Lawrence Makenroy ran his banking business from his house, which was one of the two or three finest in the Mexican city. Hewitt had not a very good acquaintance with him, and did not particularly like him. His best judgment was that he was going to have to get rough with Makenroy, and he did not really mind the prospect.

A maid told him that the señor was asleep and could not be disturbed. Hewitt's command of Spanish was colloquial but fluent, and he knew how to get along with the shy, quiet little girls who worked as servants. He had immense respect for them, because in this border town, they could have made ten or twenty times as much, plying an easier trade.

It took him fifteen minutes of earnest talk, plus another five-dollar gold piece, before the girl consented to knock on the señor's door and convey the message that Mr. Hewitt was here and must see him immediately, on a matter of many, many thousands of dollars. The girl left the door open, and Hewitt could hear the banker grumbling loudly, in his execrable Spanish. He sounded like a man with a hangover.

The girl showed Hewitt into the señor's office, a big, pleasant room with screened windows that let whatever breeze that came off the Gulf into it. He waited nearly an hour before the door opened and the banker came in.

"My God, man, I don't do business at this hour! You do have cheek, don't you, Hewitt?" he said.

Hewitt did not get up and Makenroy did not offer his hand. Hewitt nodded. "You had damn well better give thanks that I have cheek, Makenroy," he said. "I can save you a lot of money and a lot of embarrassment, but not if you come at me that way."

The banker stared at him with his bloodshot eyes full of hostility. He was probably sixty years old, a man with a naturally fine physique that had suddenly gone seedy. He had pouches under his eyes, and a pot gut. He had shaved and put on fresh clothing, but there was a faint smell of last night's liquor about him—lots of it.

Makenroy had been in Mexico for thirty years, twenty of them here in Matamoros. He had a little family income from England, but he had built up funds enough here to make him independent of his family, if it ever came to that. Hewitt, however, had never thought him a particularly good banker. He had had intelligence to begin with, but had been dependent so long on privilege that he had never learned to use it.

Hewitt had met other Englishmen like him, men from good stock that had conquered a large part of the world, but made soft by too much privilege. Makenroy exploited his aristocratic connections for all they were worth. It probably did not make him as much money as he could have made with his native intelligence, but it was easier, and far more in harmony with his station in life.

"Will you have breakfast?" Makenroy said suddenly.

"Thank you, no."

Makenroy shuddered. "Thank God for that. I don't believe I should survive the odor of food. Will you join me in coffee?"

Hewitt agreed. Makenroy hit a bell, shuddered again at its tinkle, and told the girl who answered to bring them a pot of coffee. She was back with it so quickly that Hewitt knew she had gone through this before.

Makenroy got a few swallows of coffee down. "It's such a relief to learn it hasn't killed one, isn't it?" he said, putting the coffee down. "Now perhaps I can stand to listen to you tell me how you're going to save me from some dire catastrophe."

Hewitt handed him the slick fifty-dollar gold piece. "Are you familiar with this coin?"

Makenroy examined both sides and tried to hand it back, but Hewitt left it in his hand. "Naturally I am," the banker said. "This is my business. I'm sure you know that."

"You've seen coins like that before?"

"Of course! A great number," Makenroy said irritably. "What preposterous charade is this, Hewitt?"

"You answer my questions first, and then I'll give down like the family milk cow. Have you seen many of those coins recently?"

"I'm sure I can't imagine what concern it is of yours, but naturally I have. God damn it, Hewitt, I'm a banker!"

I've got him, Hewitt thought, exultantly. . . . He said, "Would you like to have some more of them? A whole lot more? Dirt cheap, too, Makenroy. I can probably get you up to a million dollars' worth, for twenty cents on the dollar."

"*What?*" Makenroy turned the coin over and over in his hand again, and leaned toward the window to study it in better light. "This isn't counterfeit, as you might be hinting. D'you think I don't know gold?"

"Send your servant for a file and try it. There's a gold wash on there, a ten-thousandth of an inch thick. The rest is brass. Makenroy, the United States never minted many fifties, and none at all in the year shown on that. Take a better look at the engraving, for God's sake! That isn't money. It's as bogus as the charming nobleman who is going to clean you out of every cent."

Makenroy leaped to his feet and tossed the coin to Hewitt. "Not me. This isn't the sort of thing I go in for. I've a flat rule. No more than ten per cent interest, and no less than six, on a loan. No more than three per cent commission, and no less than two, on a trade or exchange. I'm a very conservative man, Hewitt. Always have been. No chances! Don't trust human nature that far. I simply don't see how—are you telling me that Kotrzina is not a count? God damn it, do you think I don't *know,* and can't *tell?*"

"Sure he's a count," Hewitt said brutally, "but he's a thief and a murderer, and he's got you fattened for the kill like a Christmas goose."

Pacing up and down, his hangover forgotten, the banker said agitatedly, "Not me, I told you. But friends of mine. Wealthy Mexican clients who trust me. And dash it, they have a right to trust me! Or always have. Wants pounds, marks, or francs. Pays double in American gold because it was minted secretly, government found itself with more gold than showed on the books, they simply corrected the books and—my God, what a story! And I believed him, Hewitt. I believed him!"

"Sit down and let's get this straight," Hewitt said soothingly. "You're buying pounds and marks and francs for him with this stuff?"

"Haven't yet. Clients are getting theirs together. Would've closed one deal yesterday, but he was in no hurry. God blast him!" Makenroy had to stop, grit his teeth, and make an effort at self-control. He went on, mopping his suddenly wet face with his handkerchief, "The bounder left a hundred of those things in my safe. Wouldn't pick up the francs yet. Said for me to keep both his gold and my client's until he got around to it."

"Until you get enough to make it worthwhile. How much are you pledged for?"

Makenroy had lost all reserve. "I've located gold enough —real gold, Hewitt!—to buy one million, six hundred and

forty thousand dollars' worth of that. I've got three hundred
thousand in my clients' money in my safe right now! And—
oh, God!—I refused to accept more than my three per cent
commission on all these transactions."

Makenroy covered his face with his hands. A good thing
I caught him hanging over, Hewitt thought. He broke down
fast and hard. . . . He said, "Pull yourself together, you
fool, and give me some help. You haven't lost anything yet.
Work with me, and you won't."

"I have to face my clients, my own friends, and tell them
—oh my God!"

"You'll have a knife between your ribs if you don't get a
grip on yourself, Makenroy. Did His Ludship ever give you
any idea where he has this miraculous hoard of bootleg
coin squirreled away?"

"No. I know his headquarters are in Austin. He represents a Frankfort banker there and—"

"He does like hell! You are able to get in touch with him
at Austin?"

"Yes, but only by telegram."

"To what address?"

"He calls for the telegrams at the station. I do the same
in Brownsville. I go there daily, as a matter of fact. We use
the code word, 'butterfly.' The agent doesn't hand over the
telegram without the password, even if he has delivered
them to us before. That's in case either of us is under duress,
you see—a hidden marksman for instance—dealing in such
enormous sums of money, we can't take any chances, don't
you know. Oh my God, what am I saying? What folly, to
be taken in by that incredible password romance!"

"How do you sign your telegrams?"

"Simply 'Milord.' To use our names, you see—"

"And how do you address yours to him?"

"To Pierre Webber. That's with two b's. He—"

"When do you expect to see him again?"

"We made a bit of a night of it together, last night. I'm rather expecting one or two clients to arrive with their francs and marks and pounds any day. He said he'll call late today, and—"

"Can you get hold of these friends, and tell them to go back and bury their gold again?"

Makenroy shook his head. "Not a chance! But let me see, let me see. I can't face this man again, I simply can't! I'll be ill when he comes. No, that won't do, not with him! I'll be called away. Death of an aunt, something like that. Stay with some people I know, near here. Have the house watched. Have the whole town watched! Moment my clients arrive, I'll catch them before they reach here, and see that they—oh my God, how can I face them?"

It was as good a plan as could be devised. One thing was sure—Makenroy did not have the cold nerve it would take to face Kotrzina and pretend he was still being fooled.

"When does he expect to return to Austin?"

"Tomorrow. An appointment he can't possibly defer."

With a shipment of brass stock, no doubt. . . . "One thing more, Makenroy—hang onto those counterfeits until I tell you—I personally—to hand them over. Let one of them get into circulation, God damn you, and I'll see that you're arrested the moment you step across that bridge."

Again Makenroy covered his face. "Don't shout at me, Hewitt. Just see that my clients don't lose anything, and I'll pay you handsomely."

"You just bet you will! My fee will be thirty thousand dollars."

"*What?*"

Haggling for an hour over the price restored some of the banker's peace of mind. They settled for fifteen thousand, and initialed an agreement to that effect.

"One thing more," Hewitt said as he departed.

"What's that?"

"Don't take a drink until I say you can."

"No chance I will," Makenroy said with a wan smile. "My God, how that man can drink! That's what did me in the eye. I'm sure one shouldn't admire men who can hold their liquor, but one does, you know. Not bright, is it?"

"Not very," said Hewitt.

CHAPTER EIGHT

Hewitt was unsaddling his horse in the stable behind the house, when Buzz Barron and Benito came out of the patio, where they had been waiting for him. A sharp spasm of alarm went through Hewitt. Buzz must have seen it in his face, for he shook his head unsmilingly.

"Everything's all right, Mr. Hewitt," he said, "but the bird has flew the coop."

"To where? Anybody know?"

Benito said, "On the train. He bought a ticket to Austin, Mr. Hewitt. Here he comes, running like hell, and got his ticket just in time to catch it. He wasn't even shaved, and when I seen him through the coach window, he was leaning back and holding his forehead. You know, like he had a bad headache."

"I think he did. When's the next train to Austin?"

"Same time tomorrow."

Buzz said, "Listen, Mr. Hewitt. I don't know if you'll understand this, but he left because he seen me."

"You mean he knew you?"

"No. Not that. I was painting trim around the side windows. He seen me when he come in on his horse, but he didn't pay no attention to me then. He puts up his horse, see, and comes back in a minute, yawning and licking his lips, to go in the house, see. He says to me, 'Going to be a hot day for that,' and I turned around politely. My first chance, you see, to get a good look at him.

"Mr. Hewitt, he takes one look at me, and I take one look at him, and we knowed each other. It's like when a new prisoner comes to the penitentiary. You only need one look at him, to know if he's been there before. Like that. One look, and he knowed I wasn't there just to paint the house. And he knowed he couldn't fool around with me, either. It'd be me or him. I don't know how to explain it, Mr. Hewitt, but—"

"You don't need to explain. I understand," Hewitt said. "How is Mrs. Frank?"

"Let me tell you. He goes on in the house, see, and I hear doors banging and him talking—not loud, but he was sure having his say. So I put my brush down and went in, and he was cursing Mrs. Frank with every raw name there is."

Hewitt could not help smiling. "And what did you do?"

"Well, sir, I said, 'You cut that kind of talk out, now,' and he cut it out and throwed his clothes into his billy-bag and started back out to the stable. Mrs. Frank tried to give him back some money, but he didn't take it and he knowed better than to say what he was thinking.

"I follered him to the barn. He had some trouble getting the saddle back on his horse. It was a fidgety horse, and he was hanging over real bad, and mighty mad. He dropped the saddle on the ground once, and next time, when he retch under the horse, he couldn't get hold of the cinch. So he throwed it over the peg and grabbed his billy-bag and started hiking."

"So he can be scared," said Hewitt.

"Yes. Anybody can be scared, but some people is worse that way than they are other times."

Hewitt thought it over for a moment. "Here's what we're going to do, Buzz. Let's figure on about forty days, painting that house. Maybe you should move in there for a while. If you run out of painting, you can find something else to do. I'm a little short of money, so we'll have to go to the bank and wait until they get the answer to a telegram."

Unless, that is, Makenroy will cash my check, he thought. I've got to see him anyway. . . . Buzz was saying, "I don't want no ten dollars a day for painting no house, and I don't want to be paid that much in advance, either. I don't need much money."

"We'll do this my way, Buzz, if you don't mind. Get on back out there and tell Mrs. Frank that you're going to be her bodyguard. Tell her I'll try to see her before I go. I'd like a chance to look through his room, so ask her not to touch it until I get there.

"Benito, I want you to meet every train from the west, and make sure he doesn't drop off on the wrong side of the train, or before it reaches the platform."

"I get my brother to help. He don't get away from us. I watch the bridge the rest of the time, when there ain't no trains in."

The same maid answered his knock, when he returned to Makenroy's house in Matamoros. This time, she admitted him immediately, without consulting Makenroy. The banker was hastily writing some letters in his office. He had shaved and was dressed for horseback.

"Now what, for heaven's sake?" he said, his face paling, when Hewitt came in.

Hewitt told him of Kotrzina's departure. "I think I know what he'll do. He's going to get hold of more bogus coins, and get back here and cash in as many as he can. I take it you don't mean to be here when he arrives."

"I couldn't face him again, Hewitt. I have never been so demoralized."

"He's a little edgy himself. I want you to send him a telegram, and give him something to worry about. Calm down, and help me compose it. Suppose that instead of being a detective, I'm an extortionist and confidence man who is trying to horn in on Kotrzina's game, how would you—"

"I'm not entirely persuaded that you're not."

Hewitt smiled. "Fine, let's proceed on that basis. You've got to have the right note of indignation, suspicion, and perhaps outrage, plus an appeal for rescue."

"All of which I feel, deeply, in my heart. It won't take me long to compose such a telegram."

"And I want you to clear me so I can cash a check for a thousand dollars in Brownsville."

"Why bother with that?" Makenroy said irritably. "I'll advance you that much on our agreement. If you don't clear up this shabby, shameful problem for me, we'll consider it a loan."

Hewitt came to the desk and leaned his weight on his hands on it. "You've got your nerve back, haven't you?"

Makenroy looked away, dreamily, for a long time. His eyes came back to meet Hewitt's at last.

"No, not really. I'm desperately fearful, but more fearful of disgrace than I am of death. You mock at the nobility— oh sir, don't deny it, I can feel your hostility! But it's not that I'm thinking about now. There has never been a hint of anything dishonest or mean or deceitful in my family's history. What I fear most is being the first to dishonor the name."

"I'm sure you know that it wouldn't be dishonesty on your part, but mere gullibility."

"Not an excuse. No one will lose anything. I can raise the money to pay off anyone whose money disappears because of me. I'm just writing my brother, to make sure he covers the claims if I'm dead."

"What are you going to do now?"

"I'll tell you, but no one else. I have a sort of private guard of my own, a dozen well-armed fighting men I can trust. They're being notified now. They'll muster south of here, and I'll join them as though we were heading toward a little cattle property I have down the coast. Instead, we'll turn west and ride like hell for Monterrey."

"I may have a better idea. Why not go across into Brownsville, and take all your money with you?"

Makenroy shuddered. "Walk right into the spider's web? Where should I hide in Brownsville?"

"In his own room, in the house where he has been staying on his visits here. Last place in the world he'll expect you. Are you any good at disguise, do you think? And will your guard be able to carry out this maneuver without you? If anyone is following them, and you, let's lead them a wild-goose chase all the way to Monterrey; only meanwhile, you're taking your ease in Brownsville, guarded by the best man I know."

"If it can be done, it would be far better than my plan," said Makenroy. "Any time a banker decamps, for whatever reason, he's fair game for thieves. I haven't liked the thought of galloping about Mexico with all my funds in gold."

I was a fool to settle for fifteen thousand, Hewitt scolded himself. Tamest banker I've ever seen. . . .

He crossed back into the United States an hour later and dismounted to chat a moment with the American border guards. A rickety wagon, badly overloaded with polewood but pulled by a spry little mustang team, came creaking across the bridge. A rangy man wrapped in a striped *serape,* with a peaked straw sombrero tilted forward to keep the sun off his face, drowsed sidewise on the load. His bare feet were filthy in their worn *huaraches,* and he smelled strongly of tequila.

Hewitt waved to him, and called, *"¡Ay! Compadre, que gusto a ver ti! ¿Cómo estás?"*

"*Cómo quiere el Dios,*" the peasant replied. "*¿Y tu?*"
"*Bien, bien!*"

"Know him?" the border guard asked.

"Oh yes! He's taking a load of wood to Mrs. Frank, where
I stay."

The guard waved the woodvender on without questions.
In a few moments, Hewitt mounted and trotted away. He
caught up with the wagon, and with a discreet nod, indi-
cated the street it should take. He ran Benito down, and
was waiting with him when the wagon arrived at Mrs.
Frank's house. He and Benito and Buzz unloaded the polewood behind the house, and helped carry the big trunk
containing all of Lawrence Makenroy's money inside.

"My, that must be heavy," said Mrs. Frank.

"Some old family keepsakes, I imagine," Hewitt said, before Makenroy could embarrass them both with some bad
lie or other. "Aunt Lettie, you're going to have to take care
of this man for a while, and he's used to service. He's a
damned British aristocrat, too old to learn new habits. Just
be as patient with him as you can."

Makenroy discarded the straw hat and *serape*, and
kicked off the sandals. "I'm not as helpless as you fancy I
am, Hewitt. I've been on this border a good many years,
now. Hoped the border and I were both past the time when
I'd have to sleep on rocks and dodge bullets, but perhaps I
was too optimistic."

"I'm afraid all there is for luncheon is beans," said Mrs.
Frank. "Fried beans and coffee, it's all I ever have for
lunch."

"I love fried beans and coffee!"

Before moving Makenroy into the room that Kotrzina
had occupied, Hewitt went through it thoroughly. He was
about to give up the search as hopeless, when he noticed a

Bible on the bedside chair. Kotrzina had not impressed him as a bedtime Bible man. He picked it up and leafed through it. There were some papers folded inside it.

The first one perplexed him. It was a carbon copy of a bill for $1,083.75 from the Peerless Smithy and Machine Works, for "steel stayplates & misc. welding, Capitol Bldg.," to what appeared to be one of the subcontractors on the new state building. There was a rent receipt from the Condon House, and a letterpress copy of a waybill to Johnson & Co., Galveston. The waybill must have been a fourth or fifth copy, because the purple indelible was hard to read. The shipment apparently had originated on the Pennsylvania and been routed eventually to the Missouri Pacific. By its date, it should have arrived a month ago.

What in the world interest had Kotrzina, in "one crated Baldwin master bleeder valve," especially one consigned to Galveston? The next one was a sheet of thin paper, covered with calculations in a tiny and beautifully clear hand, converting nine transactions in pounds, marks, and francs into $702,925 in American money.

He handed the paper to Makenroy, who merely had to glance at it before handing it back. "I hope that never becomes part of any public record, Hewitt," he said. "It's rather conclusive proof that I'm a fool, isn't it?"

"And getting out of it for fifteen thousand," said Hewitt. "Stay under cover, possess yourself in patience, and wait to hear from me. I'm going to leave Buzz Barron in command here. Better do as he advises."

"He looks dreadfully competent. Who is he?"

"A murderer who served his time."

"Exactly the man I want on my side!"

They shook hands. Benito mounted the seat of the empty wagon, to return it to a drayman in Brownsville who eventually would get it back across the border. The horse that Kotrzina had rented from the livery stable was tied on behind. Hewitt shook hands with Benito and Buzz, and kissed Mrs. Frank good-by.

At the railroad station, he bought a ticket for the next day's train, and sent three telegrams. The first went to Denny McGucken:

> MAY HAVE TO MOVE FAST STOP BELIEVE SHOULD CONFIDE IN RANGERS STOP KEEP IN TOUCH MY PARTNERS STOP URGE YOU HAVE LADY TAILED OWN PROTECTION

To Vi, he said:

> WITHOUT RISK WHO IS PEERLESS SMITHY AND MACHINE WKS STOP AUNTIE MADE MORE COOKIES THAN WE THOUGHT STOP PARTY MAY BE SURPRISE SOONEST SO WEAR BEST ALWAYS STOP SEE YOU TOMORROW

And to Johnny Quillen:

> TRY PENNSY WAYBILL NPP 57158 DATED APRIL 5 VIA MOP GALVESTON BALDWIN LOCOMOTIVE TO JOHNSON AND CO. STOP WEIGHT 175 IF READABLE STOP MAKE DENNY CALL IN RANGERS MAY NEED SOONEST SEE YOU TOMORROW

"I expect to have another one ready to go in an hour or two," Hewitt said, as the agent was computing his bill.

"I won't be here. Next trick starts before then. Barely get these on the lines, sir," the agent said curtly.

Hewitt thanked him and slid an extra two dollars across the ledge of the window. He left, and waited over his lunch until he was sure the other telegrapher would be on duty. He returned to the depot and sent the telegram that he and Makenroy had composed together. It was addressed to

Pierre Webber, care of agent, Austin, to be delivered only after identification word "Butterfly." It said:

> AMERICAN ASSERTING HE IS YOUR PARTNER DE-
> MANDING TO AUDIT ACCOUNTS STOP SAYS NAME
> IS JEFFERSON HEWITT BUT REFUSES IDENTIFY
> SELF STOP ALSO DEMANDS ONE THOUSAND CASH
> ADVANCE SMALL BILLS STOP IF YOU IN PARTNER-
> SHIP THIS TYPE I HAVE MANY MISGIVINGS AND
> REQUEST INTERVIEW SOONEST STOP IF NOT YOUR
> PARTNER WHO GAVE HIM ACCESS MY MOST PRI-
> VATE AFFAIRS QUESTION MARK STOP WARN YOU
> MUST REGARD ENTIRE ENTERPRISE IN JEOPARDY
> STOP NOT MY CUSTOM DO BUSINESS THIS FASHION
> STOP DEMAND REASSURANCE OR DEAL OFF.
>
> MILORD

"I dunno," the operator said. "I've sent one or two of these, and you ain't the man that turned them in. I ort to have some identification, or authorization, or something."

"Try this," Hewitt said, sliding a gold eagle under the paper on the ledge.

"Can't beat that. Be on its way, soon as there's a wire open to the west."

Left alone, with nothing to do for a long afternoon and an entire night, time dragged heavily for Hewitt. It was rarely hard for him to be patient, especially when there was big money at stake. But he was worried about Vi Chaney, and no longer very optimistic about collecting a record fee. The surest fees, in cases like this, came from recovering money that someone had thought gone forever.

But Lawrence Makenroy had cannily held back the flow of gold until he laid eyes on Kotrzina's, and would pay only fifteen thousand to salvage his reputation by jailing the man who had threatened it. What was still more worrisome was the chance that Kotrzina would simply pick up his precious dies, and the money already on hand, and run for it. Surely a man smart enough to plan so elaborate a swindle would have sense enough to retreat when things went against him.

I rushed into it too fast. I was too greedy, Hewitt thought, and I couldn't resist showing off to Vi. At my age, it serves me right. . . .

He found a poker game going in the livery stable, with big money on the table, and out of sheer boredom sat down in it. He began losing immediately, and lost so much, so fast, that he wondered if he were not up against one of the best sharpers in the business. Everybody else seemed to be winning, however; if there was a slicker in the game, it was not easy to identify him.

He lost a little more than three hundred dollars of the money he had got from Makenroy, before his luck turned. Night came, and Hewitt offered to send out for ham sandwiches and beer for everyone, rather than interrupt the game. He warned them that he was quitting at midnight—win, lose, or break even.

At midnight, he got up tired but refreshed, and not quite two hundred dollars winner. He slept like a baby, went to Mrs. Frank's place for breakfast after a bath and a shave, and found Buzz Barron and Lawrence Makenroy playing chess. They had been at it, Mrs. Frank said, all night.

"I thought you were painting the house," said Hewitt.

Barron, like Makenroy, was staring at the board. Neither had moved since he walked into the room. Barron did not look up.

"If this feller keeps on forcing a Russian attack," he said, "I'll hire somebody to paint the house."

"You don't play chess for money," said Hewitt. "At least, gentlemen don't."

"Gentlemen play anything for money," said Makenroy. "I won three thousand dollars one afternoon, shooting prairie chickens. He was a damned good shot, too."

"Only you were better."

"That day, I was."

They were still staring at the board when he started back to town. Neither had moved. Neither noticed him, and neither spoke.

"I'll tell them you said good-by, when they wake up," said Mrs. Frank.

"Don't bother. They won't even remember I was here. If your former star boarder shows up, you'll have to kick the board out from in front of them, to get their attention."

It was a long, hot, miserable train ride. Hewitt was standing in the vestibule, behind the conductor, when the train pulled into Austin that night. He looked about carefully before stepping down, once it stopped. There were several people on the platform, but none to cause him unease.

"Over here, Agate Eyes," came a voice.

Johnny Quillen was sitting alone in an open buggy, holding the reins of a good team with his left hand. Hewitt tossed his suitcase in the boot and got in beside him.

"Where's Vi?" he said, as Johnny turned the team expertly. Helpless in the saddle, Quillen was a horseman of professional caliber with the lines.

"Holed up in her room, scared stiff. Well, I can't say I blame her. Know what the count done tonight? Came to the hotel, bold as brass, and asked for her. Clerk said she was in. He sent a note up to her by the bellman, asking her to have dinner with him. She agreed. I guess she just about had to, if she's going to earn her pay. Anyway, I don't reckon she was scared then.

"Don't know exactly what he said or did, and I doubt she can tell you, Agate Eyes, but he just plain threw the fear of God into her. He knows she's working with us, and he said he just wanted her to know she was going to be sorry. Soon as she could, she sent word to me, and I told her to go to her room and stay there until she knew it was me or Denny McGucken outside, nobody else."

"She ought to get out of town," said Hewitt.

"I dunno. I'd rather she was here where we can keep an eye on her. That was tonight, as I say. Today, she come up with something real good. Of course, Vi has got the connections here in Austin, but I wonder if she might not learn to be a pretty fair investigator, after all."

"Let's get to the subject, Johnny. What did she get?"

"This Peerless Smithy and Machine Works does all the metal work on the new capitol building. Just about ninety days ago, it put in a lot of new machinery and machine tools, a new boiler and engine, and an office addition. Vi's informant says the machinery's the very, very best."

"German-made, at a guess," Hewitt murmured.

"Good guessin'. Everybody wondered where he got the money, because the man that owned Peerless then was a good quart-a-day man. It wasn't a foreclosure—that'd take too long. However it was done, Peerless has a new owner now."

"Let me see if I can guess who."

"While you're guessing, my own guess is that he just put a few hundred dollars in this poor old drinking blacksmith's hand, and a gun in his back."

"Or a knife."

"I stand corrected. Another thing, that was a good tip you had on the locomotive valve. It was checked into a unit car at St. Louis that was consigned straight through to

Galveston. It never turned up there. And you know what else?"

"Consignee never filed a loss claim."

"Right! This scaper wasn't going to be seen taking in no such freight by daylight in Texas. No idee where he went into the car and helped himself, but it was about the right length."

"Damn! I'd sure like to get a look in that blacksmith shop."

"Nothing to see tonight, but I'll let you see it tomorrow. There's a vacant dray stable next door to it. I bought a good carpenter's brace and expansion bit, and bored myself a couple of inch-and-a-half holes in the wall, so you can see into the shop from the dray stable. They ain't likely to be noticed from inside the shop. Tonight, once I find out where Kotrzina is, I'm going to try to bore a couple from the alley into the office.

"Office adjoins the shop, and they say there's a locked, windowless storage room about sixteen feet square, that opens only into the office. All Vi and I was able to pick up, so far.

"But from my peepholes into the shop, I could see a one-inch steam line that ran straight from the boiler in the shop, into the back end of that office building. There, I'll just about bet you, is where his minting press is. Steam powered. Ain't no better cover for it than a blacksmith shop, and damned if he ain't making money on the shop, too!

"Another thing, I picked up one thing from one of the teamsters in the dray outfit that used to hang out in the shop under the old owner. Nobody hangs out there now. The feller tells me one of the new power machines is a high-speed hacksaw that uses a two-inch-wide, Number Thirty-six blade. Maybe you know what that means."

"Thirty-six teeth to the inch."

"Oh. Well, he said he seen the pieces of a busted blade on the scrap pile the other day. A different blade. Three-quarters of an inch wide, a sixty-fourth of an inch thick, and about a Number Fifty. He says he never seen a blade like that used on a big saw like Peerless has got, but it would sure be great if it worked, for certain jobs."

"Like slicing soft brass stock without waste, about as fast as you can slice cheese. And if it's got an automatic feed—"

"Oh, it has, it has! You want I should go up with you to Vi's room?"

They had stopped in front of the Condon House. "By all means," Hewitt said heartily. There was nothing that he wanted less.

They went upstairs together, Hewitt carrying the key to his own room, as well as his suitcase. He put the suitcase down near Vi's door, while Johnny knocked softly. She was so long answering, that Hewitt felt a moment of panic.

"Yes?" she said at last.

"It's me, Johnny. I brung our friend here from the train."

The bolt was shot back, the key was turned, and the door opened quickly, if cautiously. Vi's hand came out and caught him by the wrist, to draw him inside. She threw herself against him, shivering. He put his arms around her and said, "Hold on, here! What kind of a detective are you?"

"A scared kind," came her muffled voice. "Let's get it over with. That man's crazy! Unless he's killed or locked up, he's going to do something awful. And I'm afraid I'll be the one. My God, Jeff, what a monster!"

Hewitt looked over her head at Johnny, who shrugged. "Either she's scared real bad, Agate Eyes, or she likes that huggin'."

Vi looked up. "Both," she said.

CHAPTER NINE

Monty, the head waiter, was sent to Denny McGucken's hotel to call him. They waited for him in Vi's room. "He notified me that he's taking personal charge of the case," Johnny said. "He said nobody is to do anything without first clearing it with him."

"Now all he has to do is make his bluff good," said Hewitt.

"You figger to ignore that?"

"If we have to. If we choose to. Denny's a good man, Johnny, and we want to co-operate with the government. But let's never forget that it's our case."

Johnny looked dubious. "He's pretty mad at you already. I don't even know if he'll come here, when he knows it's Vi's room. He is dead against women in this kind of business."

Hewitt began pacing the floor restlessly. "Let's get one thing straight before he gets here. All we have to do is walk out of the case, taking what we know with us, and they're up the tallest tree in Texas. You're going to tell me that three humble citizens can't talk eye-to-eye with the United States government. Well, I'm telling you that *one* person already is doing just that—Count Kotrzina. Every case eventually comes down to a showdown between two persons, doesn't it, Johnny?"

"I guess that's right."

"You know it's right! And I'm an old hand at the game

of man hunting, and so are you. So is Denny McGucken—don't forget that he used to be a cop. So we're going to stick together on this, and either the Treasury does business our way, or they can start over again and work the case up from the beginning."

"You sound very cocksure," said Vi.

Hewitt shook his head. "Not cocksure, just money-hungry. I know by now that there isn't much of this stuff in circulation. We're not going to be able to recover from the losses of suckers, because there haven't been any suckers except the ones we already know about. Unless Uncle Sam pungles up, we're working cheaply."

He told them rapidly but in detail about Lawrence Makenroy, and the agreement he had reached with him. He had barely finished when there was a knock at the door, and he nodded to Vi to open it.

She had paled suddenly. "No, you open it," she whispered. "If it's the count—oh Jeff, what if it is?"

He shook his head impatiently, but opened the door with one hand on his gun. Denny McGucken, alone, was waiting in the hall. Hewitt let him in, and then closed and locked the door again.

"Where are your two faithful shadows, Pikus and Asbury?" Hewitt asked him without any other greeting.

"Sleeping in their clothes, just in case we have to go into action suddenly," the Treasury man replied. "What's new in the case, Jeff?"

"What's new from the Secretary, first?"

Hewitt was amazed to see McGucken fumble in his pocket until he found a yellow telegram, which he handed over silently. It was directed to Denny, that much was clear. It was signed CENTENNIAL, and the message itself was obviously in code: ABRUPTLY LOCALITY PERSIMMON CULT SAMARITAN VERIFY DOUBLE VERIFY.

Hewitt handed the wire back to McGucken, who jammed it carelessly back in his pocket and leaned against the wall, for lack of a place to sit.

"The Secretary approves thirty thousand dollars," he said.

Hewitt was able to repress the sudden feeling of glee that he felt, but Johnny and Vi both gasped delightedly. McGucken went on:

"The reward is contingent upon laying our hands on the counterfeiter, his equipment and dies, and the coins he has made so far. That was your proposition, and that's what I put to him, and that's what he's accepting. So much for that. But he also authorizes me to disclose to you what we know about this case ourselves—on agreement of course that it remains confidential."

Hewitt, Vi and Johnny all nodded, and McGucken went on to tell them the story.

A little over a year ago, the Secretary had received in the mail a small, rather heavy parcel wrapped in heavy brown paper. It was opened by someone on his staff, and taken into the Secretary's private office immediately. The small box inside contained ten gold slicks.

The letter accompanying it offered to sell the dies to the Treasury for three million dollars. If the offer was not accepted within six months, the world would be flooded with counterfeit American fifty-dollar gold pieces. They would be put into circulation all over the globe—twenty million dollars within three months, fifty million in the next three.

"The letter, which I have seen, pointed out that the writer knew he could not possibly sell that much counterfeit gold," said McGucken. "But he declared that he had already arranged to sell enough to leave him with a couple of million profit. He would make the rest of the counterfeit issue at his own expense, and give them away if necessary—anything to get them into the world money markets."

"He didn't lack for cheek, as Lawrence Makenroy would say. The time limit obviously has expired. Then what happened?" Hewitt said.

"This isn't the kind of decision the government should make alone. The Secretary called in twelve of the biggest bankers in the country. Now here is the ominous thing—eight of them had already detected these counterfeits in their own vaults, and were deeply concerned about it. The counterfeiter had furnished a code name, 'Samaritan,' so they could get in touch with him through a classified ad in any New York newspaper," said McGucken.

"The bankers formed an emergency committee, and placed an ad offering to negotiate with Samaritan. To make a long story short, they did negotiate for several months, and ended up taking fifty thousand dollars in slicks at the counterfeiter's own price of ten thousand dollars."

"You mean they closed a deal? How did this chap receive the ten thousand?"

McGucken smiled wryly. "He specified only that it was to be brought to a certain concert in Philadelphia, a very fine German soprano, where an aisle seat in the seventh row was reserved for him. About all we can deduce with any certainty is that the counterfeiter was somewhere behind the seventh row, where he could keep the messenger with the ten thousand under observation.

"Of course, the place was full of Secret Service agents and cops, thirty of them, to tell the truth. They had just about given up any hope that the man would try to make contact with them. The artist was in her second encore when it happened—an explosion in the boiler room in the basement. No need to tell you the rest."

"Fire broke out," said Hewitt, "everybody stampeded for

the exits, and the man with the coin was relieved of it in the rush."

"Exactly! Knocked unconscious—never knew how!—and the next thing he knew, he was in the hospital, where he spent the next twenty days."

"Did the fellow make good on delivery of the slicks?"

"Oh yes. They were shipped by express that same day. They arrived on Wall Street two days later. Now, here is an interesting thing."

"Let me guess," said Hewitt. "The first coins sent to the Secretary were hand-stamped, slugged out with a sledge hammer. The fifty thousand dollars' worth were machine-made."

"Exactly. Since then, we have naturally been very concerned, which is why—"

"Two more questions, Denny. First, how was the Secretary to pay off the three million, if the decision was made to take him up on the deal?"

"A draft for that amount, signed by the Secretary himself, was to be delivered to a minor official in the office of the Chancellor of the Empire in Berlin. It was to be accompanied by a letter, also signed by the Treasurer, stating that the money was in payment of a just claim that the payee had against the United States. Naturally, we would hardly be in a position, after that, to ask the German foreign office to arrest the man who came to claim the draft. The minor official in the Chancellery, by the way, was discreetly interviewed."

"And I'll bet he was related to the Kotrzinas."

Again that twisted, unhappy smile. "That was his own name, in fact. He's an elderly career man, very proud of his distant kinship to the aristocratic Kotrzina family, and completely innocent. What's your other question?"

"Suppose that, when we jump on the count and arrest

him and lay hands on his equipment, we also recover a
good part of the ten thousand laid out by the Samaritan
committee—how much of that do we keep?"

"None, I'm afraid. That's included in your deal for the
thirty thousand dollars in reward money."

"I was afraid of that." Hewitt sighed. He avoided looking
at either Johnny or Vi. "We've got to have a look at this
minting works of his, and we need a peephole. I think
that's our first order of business—make sure he's not on the
premises, and let Johnny in with his brace and bit. But to
make sure he's not at the Peerless Smithy, we almost have
to know where he is."

McGucken said, "He has been calling every night recently at a—a—well, shall we call it an establishment, for
lack of a better word? It's known as Bessie's Place, and I'm
told that they serve some very good food and wine there,
if you're one of a distinguished inner circle."

"And the hostesses are all lovely and ladylike," Hewitt
murmured. "I'm sure we don't just go there and knock and
ask for him, do we?"

"No. He has acquired a team and phaeton, and a coachman to drive them. Hugh Pikus was watching Bessie's Place
this evening. As soon as the count's rig appeared, he came
back to the hotel and went to bed. The count rarely leaves
there before two or three in the morning."

"Then I suggest that we first verify that his rig is still
waiting for him," said Hewitt. "I'll stay with that watch,
while Johnny bores his peephole."

"You feel the peephole is necessary?" said McGucken.

"Denny, I know enough about this fellow now to put
him in the salthouse for the rest of his life, but you want to
go into court with a perfect case, don't you? You want to
be able to put witnesses on the stand, who can testify that
they actually saw coins being made, don't you?"

McGucken looked at him a long time. "I'll agree that the peephole would help our case, Jeff, but somehow I have an uneasy feeling that while you're giving me that frank and innocent look, I'm having my pockets picked."

"Denny, I promise you that you're going to make your Secretary happy. Suppose you go verify the count's aristocratic presence at Bessie's Place—and you, Johnny, go get your brace and bit. I'll wait here for you."

The two men went out. Vi sat down on the edge of the bed again. "I'm not scared stiff any more," she said, "but Jeff, don't underestimate the count! He must be the most dangerous man in the world. You're good at any kind of fighting, I'm sure. But for one thing, he'll outweigh you by forty pounds. And he's worse than a madman. He's a fanatic, like a man who believes he can be killed only by a silver bullet."

Hewitt said, "No question about it, he's tough. But he's not as bad as you and Johnny and Denny seem to think. That's part of his procedure, Vi—to throw terror into everybody he deals with. The only response to that is merely to refuse to be terrorized."

"Wait till you're face to face with him!"

"I'll find that he pulls his pants on one leg at a time, like all the rest of us. Overestimating an adversary is as dangerous as underestimating one, Vi."

She cocked her head to study him. "You're a sort of fanatic yourself, you know that? There's not a bit of brag in you, and yet you're the most self-confident man I have ever met."

"I've been a man hunter for half my life, and I've known one thing for most of that time. Which is, that any man who steps outside the law to make his way in the world, is admitting that he can't compete under the rules the rest of us live up to. He can be a maniac or a fanatic or anything else, and he can be very dangerous indeed. But he is still a man with a defect that makes him noncompetitive, and that's a very big defect. Any man with that kind of defect, I can handle," he said slowly.

She got up and crossed the room to him. She fit herself against him in the way of a woman who expects a man to put his arm around her. He put his arm around her, and she snuggled against him with a contented sigh. He heard her say:

"Nobody can patronize me just because I'm a woman—nobody! I can do any job that a man can do, and I've proved it lots of times. But sometimes it's nice just to relax and feel someone is protecting me."

"Just remember that the fellow you're hunting often wishes he had someone to protect him," Hewitt said. "This Kotrzina has many a lonesome, frightened, unhappy moment, and don't you ever forget it!"

"That, I will never believe. Wait till you see him!"

She was so serious that he could not help a twinge of doubt. He had heard of so many "master" criminals, men who supposedly had put themselves above the law because of superior intelligence. He had hunted down a few, and all had proved to be merely smart, tough, and overconfident. Their "genius" was mostly egotism.

Yet, every now and then he had wondered what would happen if a truly superior intellect was ever dedicated to crime. Geniuses *did* exist. He had met a few himself. One was a mathematician who could mentally extract the cube root of 456,533, and come out with 77 before you could do the first multiplication with a pencil. He had known a girl by the name of Helen, who had never heard a piano player until she was eighteen. She sat down to it after hearing a fine pianist play it, fooled around with the keys a few minutes, and soon was repeating the pianist's music with absolute fidelity. In three days more, she was playing and sight-reading the most complex piano scores.

What if someone like that set out on a career of crime? Suppose, for instance, he decided to skip what might be termed the "retail" level of crime—ordinary people with money in their pockets or in the bank—and even "wholesalers" like the banks. Suppose he went straight to the source of all wealth, government itself, and *proved in advance* that he could wreck its credit and make its money worthless?

Why stop at three million dollars? Why not use that three million to finance an assault on every government on earth? Why not eventually *be* the government, controlling millions upon uncounted millions of people, through control of their currencies? Let them have their armies, their navies, their police forces—so long as his secret mint remained, he still ruled them.

It was a dismaying thought, unless your own life had proved that even a genius put his pants on one leg at a time. Hewitt, who did not claim to be brilliant, and who knew he was far from being a genius, would not have been at all surprised to learn that Count Kotrzina dreamed just such dreams. And he still felt fairly confident of beating him.

"One thing," Vi said.

"What?"

"Why are you so concerned about a peephole? We know where the coins are struck. Why not just sail in and put him out of business?"

He tilted her chin up with his hand. "When you've been in the man-hunting business as long as I have, my dear, you learn that catching your man is only the first half of the job. After that, you've got to collect. This fellow has made off with a lot of money, a big lot of it! Much of it has gone on expenses. But he still has a fund of cash on hand, I feel sure. He needs real money to make his getaway. If his dream of shaking three million out of the Treasury fails him, he still means to come out winner."

"How?"

"He'll hold back some real cash, believe me. If it's found on the premises, the government will grab it and pay off the Samaritan committee first. Our clients are going to have to go into court and prove that they didn't have larceny in their hearts, to recover their losses—and I don't think they can do it. I want a good look at his place before we raid it, so I can levy on it before the Treasury. Otherwise, we're going to be short on our fee."

A knock at the door, and Johnny Quillen's low voice outside interrupted them. He let Johnny in, carrying his brace and bit in a brown paper sack.

"Denny's in Volney's saloon, where he can watch Bessie's Place. The rig is still at the curb, but the count came down and spoke to the coachman a few minutes ago. Denny's afraid he's going to be leaving soon," he reported.

"Then," said Hewitt, "I had best go see that he doesn't. How do I find Volney's saloon?"

"I'll show you."

Vi said, "I can tell you about his rig. The team is a good one, matched chestnuts that used to belong to a retired cattleman and banker. The phaeton is quite old. It—it used to be in my husband's family. It has been repainted, black with yellow wheels. It wouldn't cause much stir in New York, probably, but it's impressive here. The coachman, though, is really just the town drunk. His name is Byron Sutton. No real harm in him, except that his family goes hungry while he drinks up everything he makes. Oh yes— the horses' names are Jenny and Opal."

He pinched her cheek. "And you're just the town gossip, aren't you? You really should become a detective."

She slapped his hand away. They went out, and waited until she had bolted the door behind them. They went downstairs and walked two blocks. Johnny stopped and pointed.

"Yander, around that corner, and one block down—that's Volney's, if it's still open," he said. "Bessie's Place is across the street, only two-story building in the block. She has the whole upstairs. Stairway door don't look like much, but they tell me it's a real palace at the top of the steps," he said.

They parted. Hewitt walked on. He passed Volney's saloon, and a man came to the door without looking at him and went back inside. It was Denny McGucken. Hewitt crossed the street and walked on.

Even in the dark, the new enamel on the phaeton seemed to glitter. The horses moved their feet continuously, the only way they could protest the tight checkreins that held their heads high, in the stylish posture favored by fashion. The coachman, who wore worn Levi's and a ragged, sleeveless shirt, leaned against the wheel with the whip in his hand. Every now and then, he tapped its butt impatiently on the sidewalk, like a man needing a drink.

Hewitt stopped and patted one of the horses on the back. "I know this team, don't I?" he said. "Their names are Jenny and Opal, I believe."

"Don't bother the horses," the coachman said.

"I'm not bothering them, but you are. Don't you know that there's a Texas law prohibiting cruelty to horses? And that the courts have held that so tight a checkrein is cruelty under the act? You could go to jail for this."

The coachman merely thumped the pavement harder with his whip. Hewitt reached up and unsnapped the horse's checkrein. He went swiftly around the team, and unsnapped the other checkrein. The way the horses tossed their heads, relieving the ache in their cramped necks, was almost as clear as a spoken "Thank you."

When he came back around in front of the teams, he saw the coachman snapping the first checkrein up again. "I told you," Hewitt said, "that we don't treat horses like that in Texas."

He took out his pocket knife and opened it. He pushed the coachman aside with his shoulder, and cut the checkrein. He hurried around to the other horse, and cut its checkrein too.

He returned to the sidewalk, ready to come inside the whip and close with the coachman. The man was just standing there. "Cruel, it is—cruel, cruel!" he was saying. "I've never before mistreated a horse like that. It only shows you how low the drink can bring you."

"Yes," said Hewitt, "and it's too bad when a dumb beast has to pay for it."

"The horses is not the worst. There's my family, too. My wife and oldest daughter taking in washing to buy food for the table that I eat."

"Only one answer to that."

"You mean quit drinking." When Hewitt did not answer, the man ran his hand down the horse's sleek shoulder. "So simple, just to cut the checkrein, and I never did it. Ah dear, here comes the count, and I'm jobless again."

The man who came out of the blank stairway door was close to six feet four, Hewitt estimated. He had adapted to Texas clothing, but he had spent a lot of money on his black broadcloth coat, light tan trousers, fawn-colored, ten-gallon hat and black boots. He wore spurs of real silver, and a silver watch chain twinkled behind the opening of the fine coat.

Big, flat, pallid face, with a flat nose. Mouth full and

feminine-looking. Cheeks as smooth as a boy's. Long, square jaw, and a long upper lip with a deep cleft in it. The madness of a madman rarely showed on his face in daylight, and this was late at night on a dark street. But Hewitt thought, Oh, but doesn't he think he's some punkins! And I know I've whipped better. . . .

"Are you Kotrzina?" he said.

"I am Count Kotrzina, yes." The man came to a stop, watchfully. "Who are you?"

"The name is Hewitt."

A moment of silence.

"Ah yes, and you've just come from Matamoros, I'm sure," the count said. "You're a fool, you know."

"Not really. We'll go into that some other time. I just want to call your attention to your harness, now. I have cut both checkreins, as you see. You're not allowed to mistreat a horse in Texas."

"Thank you," said the count. "I'm sure you think of yourself as a dangerous man, Hewitt. In this frontier environment, you may well be celebrated. But please don't insult me with any of your Texas bluff! Now get out of my way, or I shall have to teach you a lesson."

"It isn't a bluff, you four-flusher. I came here to beat the living hell out of you. Are you going to fight back, or crawl on your belly like a whipped dog?"

"I understand now. Why, my God, you've talked to Mrs. Chaney! You imagine I'll fight you like a gentleman over a riffraff country widow!"

And this, Hewitt thought, is where I'm supposed to lose my head and start swinging. And just for that, I will. . . . He said, "You son of a bitch!" and put all the feeling he could into it. He charged Kotrzina with both fists doubled up, his head down.

Kotrzina had done some boxing. He stuck out his left,

and Hewitt slid into it glancingly and hooked with his own left. He missed and then got his head out of the way as Kotrzina shot two short right jabs at him. A boxer, yes, but not a fist fighter. Boxing was something every nobleman learned, the same as he learned the waltz and the schottische. For combat to the kill, Kotrzina's type wanted a weapon.

Hewitt feinted once with his left and once with his right. He caught Kotrzina in the belly then with a left, landing more solidly than he had hoped. He knew Kotrzina would go for his weapon then, and he did. Hurt one of these headstrong egotist types, and you were inviting the killer to come out fast.

Hewitt's hand dropped to his hip pocket and came out with the shot-filled, leather sap that was his favorite weapon. He timed it to land on the wrist when Kotrzina got the knife out. It was a short, wide, double-edged blade, and the count was a belly cutter. He carried the knife low, like a sword, and he took the sap on the soft inside of his wrist.

The knife tinkled to the pavement. Hewitt caught Kotrzina's coat and swung him into the sap, which caught him lightly over the mouth. Kotrzina's knees buckled, and Hewitt brought his knee up into the man's crotch and then threw his weight against him.

They went down together, Hewitt on top. "I could knock your brains out, you poor stupid son of a bitch," he panted, "but I want you conscious when I do this to you. I want to know that you know what's happening. This is for Doc Nolan, to start with."

He got his left hand on Kotrzina's wrist and spread Kotrzina's hand flat on the sidewalk. He hit it savagely, twice, with the sap. Kotrzina broke loose and Hewitt had to tap him on the side of the head again, to quiet him. He held the other hand on the sidewalk and rapped it twice with the sap, before standing up.

He picked up the knife as he got to his feet, and tried the blade with his thumbnail. "English, isn't it?" he said. "Good edge, but isn't it a little out of balance? If you don't know how to make it right, ask a Cuban. I learned to use a knife from a Cuban. I'd have cut my initials in you, while you were getting this out. You're not very good at this, Kotrzina. In fact, you're not much good at anything, are you? And both of us know it, don't we?"

Kotrzina was dazed and in pain, but was perfectly conscious. He sat up, leaning on both hands. His hat had fallen off, and the silky, blond hair around his bald spot was comically in disarray. He was not going to get up and try it again—not tonight—and Hewitt knew it.

He tossed the knife down beside Kotrzina, and turned and started back toward the Condon House. He thought he heard Kotrzina calling him and turned a moment.

"How's that?"

"Stay out of my affairs," Kotrzina said, getting slowly to his feet. "I will not stand for interference, and next time, I will not be drawn into a street fight."

Hewitt ignored him and walked on. At Volney's, Denny McGucken was leaning in the doorway. "What was that all about?" he said.

"Just sizing him up," Hewitt replied. "I like to know what I'm dealing with, Denny."

"What was your conclusion?"

"Hell of a man, when he's fighting a woman. You would break him in pieces."

"Maybe, maybe. You were to keep him occupied until Quillen got his hole bored."

"Johnny's on his way home by now. You don't know him as well as I do, Denny."

"What will happen now?"

"He's got to start producing coins. His hand has been forced—yes, and beaten a little, too—both of them. I just wonder how nimble those fingers of his are going to be, on a die-stamp press or anything else, after the beating I gave them."

"The fellow's almost a mythical monster, in the Treasury Department."

"Myths are easy to whip, Denny. It's when a *man* comes at you that you've got your hands full. All of you have made the same mistake. This fellow is only human."

"Maybe, maybe. Look, he's driving his own rig!"

Kotrzina was handling, with some difficulty, the lines of his fine chestnut team as it went down the street away from them, at a smart trot. The suddenly retired coachman, Byron Sutton, watched the receding rig for a moment. As Hewitt told McGucken good night, and headed back toward the Condon House, Sutton came after him.

He caught him at the hotel door. "Excuse me a minute, sir. I've lost my job because of you," he said.

"And now you want me to pay you," said Hewitt.

"Not for that. I know a thing or two about His Nibs, though, that it might pay you to know too. I'd have three dollars and a half coming to me, this night. If you could see your way clear to paying that to me—"

"Why? The saloons are all closed. What good is money to you?"

"Not to drink, sir. To take home to my wife."

"At this hour? Then she'll know you're drunk!"

"She'll think so, anyway. Until I open her dear hand and put the money in it. I—I think I could quit now. It was good to see, sir, the way you beat the hell out of the count. And there are some things about him that should be made known to the police, only who am I to tell them? Just a drunk, a sot, a swinish derelict. Who'd believe me?"

"How much did you say he owed you?"

"Three and a half, sir, but I'd be grateful for—"

"Mr. Sutton, here's a five-dollar bill. You could take your full wages home to your wife, and still have enough to get drunk on. See me tomorrow, stone sober, and we'll talk about the other. You see, Mr. Sutton—I don't believe what a drunk says, either!"

CHAPTER TEN

Hewitt awakened at daylight, and lay naked on the bed with his hands locked behind his head, thinking, for a long time. It was going to be another hot, humid day. What should have been a fairly routine case—big, but still routine —had been complicated by the almost superstitious awe that Kotrzina had inspired in everyone. The more he thought about it, the surer Hewitt was that the count was a hollow man, a bluffer, a cavern of self-doubts in which the cold, strong winds of apprehension blew endlessly. You did not have to beat a man like that. All you had to do was mock him and goad him into beating himself.

Thirty minutes later, freshly shaved, mustache carefully trimmed, and in fresh clothes that would not stay fresh long in this weather, he knocked on Vi's door. She let him in, and then locked the door behind him. A man could forget how pretty she was, and it was a stimulating surprise to be reminded at this hour of the morning.

They went out and down the stairs together to the dining room, which had just opened. Johnny Quillen and Denny McGucken were already at Hewitt's favorite table, waiting for their coffee.

McGucken opened the conversation with a question. "Jefferson, you had Kotrzina at your mercy last night, and I thought you let him off easy. Why?"

The waiter brought cups and a big jug of coffee. Hewitt waited until he had taken their orders and gone.

"I banged his hands up a little. We're pretty sure that he's got to start striking more coins in a hurry. The harder we bear down on him, the more urgent it is for him to get some coins out, so he can do business with somebody. It's not going to be easy for him to do it, with both hands bunged up, that's all," he said.

Denny gritted his teeth. "I talked it over with George Flowers. Much as we'd like to catch him with a lot of coins on hand—"

Hewitt cut in. "Who is George Flowers?"

"The new superintendent of the Texas Rangers. Can't come in here and not take the Rangers into your confidence, and George is the best, tough and smart and experienced. As I was saying, I wish we could catch him with the booty, of course. But I get cold chills whenever I think of him getting away with those dies, while we're waiting to make our move. I'd like to hit him today, and George agrees."

"You aren't sure—at least I'm not—that he has the dies in the blacksmith shop," said Hewitt. "If we raid him, and find they're hidden somewhere else, he has the rest of his life to use them. Let's not make up our minds until later in the day. I hope to pick up some more information on him today."

No one spoke for a moment. Then Vi said, "From whom?"

"From your town drunk, Byron Sutton."

She frowned and shook her head. "I don't think you can count on anything he tells you, Jeff. I've known him ever since I was a little girl, and he has always been completely unreliable."

"You would rather raid now?"

She nodded. "Anything to get him in jail!"

"What if you have to let him out again?" She did not

answer. He looked at Johnny and McGucken. "You feel the same way?"

Johnny said, "Agate Eyes, those dies are in that office. Well, not in the office, probably, but in that locked room behind it. Where else would they be?"

"Johnny, you're probably right, that's where they are. But I say we have to have the patience to be sure. We're dealing with a man who has been patient for several years. Just when we've put enough pressure on him to make him rush things, you want to get as impatient as he is. It's just not my way of doing things."

McGucken pounded the table lightly with his big fist. "But if we depend on the word of a drunk, and he turns out to be as unreliable as Mrs. Chaney says—"

Hewitt took his roll of currency from his pocket, and peeled off three one-hundred-dollar bills. "Anybody want to bet me even money that my drunk is unreliable? Money talks, gentlemen."

McGucken ignored the currency. "Jefferson, I can't consent to any further delay, and I'm in charge of this case."

Hewitt leaned across the table and said, *"You're* in charge of it? *You're* in charge? Denny, you're riding double on my horse. You and your whole damned department have been floundering around like a shark in a bath tub for over a year. I found this fellow, I found the circulated coins, I ran him down, and I say we wait until we know more about it before we pull a raid."

"The Secretary will never stand for—"

"The Secretary will sit on his duff in his office until Johnny and Vi and I decide it's time for him to be told the facts. You're a lawyer now, Denny. You used to be a cop, but you have forgotten how it's done."

After a moment, Denny said, "No, I haven't. But I can't forget that I've got to account to the Secretary, and he has to account to the President. All right, another day won't matter that much. But I'm going to ask Colonel Flowers to keep men in that dray stable next door, and to have someone tail the suspect wherever he goes."

"Fair enough." Hewitt turned to Johnny Quillen. "How about the peepholes—don't they help us at all?"

"Only way to see into the little room behind the office was to go through the smithy wall. That's what I did. I ain't worried about him seeing the hole, but the place was darker than a yard down a cow's throat last night. We can't see anything until he makes a light in there."

"Which he'll have to do, to start producing coins. Here comes our breakfast. Are we friends?"

"I reckon." Johnny sighed. "But it's like always—friends on your terms. Someday I'm going to catch you with a buckle unbuckled, and I'll grind your face in the dirt."

They ate. Johnny had to see Dr. Chaney to have his dressing changed and his stitches seen to. Vi went with Denny McGucken to break the news to Colonel George Flowers that there would be no raid today. It did not surprise Hewitt to learn that she had known him since she was a little girl, and Flowers was then a young lieutenant who, single-handed, had just brought in a killer who had terrorized three counties for a year.

Hewitt waited until the other three had gone before showing himself in the lobby. Sure enough, Kotrzina's former coachman was lounging near the hotel door, leaning against the wall with his ankles crossed. Hewitt came close enough to the door to get his attention.

"In the bar," he said in a low voice.

Sutton might not have heard, for all the notice he gave; but in a moment he straightened up and shambled toward the corner, around which was the family entrance of the

Condon House saloon. He walked with his head down, his hands in his pockets, with the uncertain steps of a man who had long lived on intimate terms with the bottle.

Hewitt went through the hallway that effectively insulated the saloon from the hotel lobby. The barroom was deserted. The solitary barkeep was reading a dime Wild West novel by the light of an overhead lamp. He put the book down when he saw Hewitt, and lighted another lamp.

"It's purely wonderful," he said.

"What is?" said Hewitt.

"What writers write about Texas. This'n's got a two-gun bandit who says 'Curses!' every time he gets mad. I never heard nobody talk that way. This'n's always drinking rum punch, too. Bourbon's what they drink here, but I got a recipe that makes a good rum punch. Nobody ever orders it, but I know how to make it."

"Let's prove that truth is stranger than fiction, shall we? I'll have a rum punch."

The bartender nodded solemnly and mixed the drink. "Here you are, sir."

Hewitt hoisted the glass in a toast. "Curses," he said.

"That's just wonderful. Now I know you're a real two-gun man." The bartender looked up as Byron Sutton came in the street door. He watched him make for Hewitt. "This fellow can be a problem when he's drinking," he said, dropping his voice. "If he annoys you, I'll send him on his way."

"He won't annoy me. We're friends."

Sutton no longer shambled along with his head down. He leaned against the bar beside Hewitt.

"I'm stone sober," he said defiantly.

"I thought you would be."

"I gave my wife that money."

"And now you want more."

"Yes, and by God, it's worth it! You went to all the

trouble of boring them peepholes, you want to know what's going on in there mighty bad."

Hewitt felt a little let down. "Does the count know about the peepholes?"

"No. Fur as I know, I'm the only one."

"How do you know about them?"

Sutton grinned. "I seen your friend bore them. One thing about being the town drunk, nobody's surprised to see you anywhere, and nobody pays any attention to you when they do."

"Sutton, what's going on in that room?"

"I don't know, and that's the truth. But the count don't plan to be caught doing it, you can bet on that! He finished that little room his own self. Nobody's been in it since the door was hung—only him. And there ain't going to be nobody go in, either!"

"Why not?"

"He's got a ten-gauge shotgun rigged, to go off with both barrels, minute that door is opened. He sets it when he leaves, and it takes a key to disarm it when he wants to go in again. When he's working there, he sets with his back to the door. But he's got a little rope rigged, and a mirror to watch the door. All he has to do is give that rope a tug, and both barrels go off."

Plenty of reason not to pull a raid without knowing what we're raiding, Hewitt thought. . . . "Anything more you think I ought to know?"

"Well. . . . The count lives in a little house of his own, you know. He started to buy furniture for it, but he called it off last week. All he's got there is a bed and a chest of drawers. Mr. Hewitt, is this worth anything to you? I've got a good start on beating the rum, but if you get the name of a drunkard, jobs are hard to come by. If I could just have some money to hand the wife—"

"I don't want the bartender to see me paying you. Where can I leave it for you?"

Sutton looked at him suspiciously, but consented. He went out. Hewitt finished his drink, saluted the bartender, and took the street door too. "Curses," the bartender said, in reply. Hewitt dropped ten ten-dollar bills behind the spittoon that stood just inside the door, and went out into the street.

Sutton was not in sight, but a little later, Hewitt saw him marching along with his head back, his shoulders straight. No doubt he had every intention in the world of hurrying home with the money, but it was at least ten to one that he would get sidetracked in a saloon before he ever got there. Well, Hewitt thought, ten to one is pretty good odds, and a man has to make that kind of a bet once in a while. I'll pick the wife to get the money. . . .

He went up to his room and stretched out on the bed. He had dozed off comfortably, when someone knocked sharply at the door. He got up in his sock feet and opened it on an excited Johnny Quillen.

"Get your boots on, Agate Eyes. We raid," Johnny said.

"Why?" said Hewitt.

"He's slicing off blanks with that high-speed saw. Whole blacksmith crew was sent home this morning, and paid for a full day's work, by God, so they'd go home and stay! Me and Denny and George Flowers have been taking turns watching through the peephole from the stable. Smithy is locked up tighter than your ulcerated ear. Denny timed it, and he's slicing off a blank every ten seconds!"

Hewitt sat down on the bed and yawned. "And then what's he doing with them? How is it against the law to cut off pieces of brass? What's going on in the little secret room off the office? Where are the dies?"

Johnny said harshly, "Goddamn it, he ain't cutting that

brass up to make tiepins. The dies are in the little room
somewhere. If we kick in the door now—"

"No. You'll never find the dies. And if you wait until
he's locked into the little room, everybody that tries to go
in the door will be blown to smithereens. This isn't like you,
Johnny—to get so excited, just when we most need to keep
cool."

He told Johnny about the shotgun that had been rigged
to kill any one—or any two, or any three, or any four—who
kicked in the door from the office. "We've got to wait until
he has the dies in the press, and is striking coins, Johnny.
And then we've got to figure out some way to go in there
and take him, without being ground up for mincemeat by
that double-barreled ten."

"Hell!" Johnny sat down heavily. "At least, come over
and see for yourself. I don't know anything about machinery, and neither do Denny and George Flowers. He puts
the blanks in some kind of a spinning barrel, as soon as a
pile of them have been cut up. And he sure is laying in a
big supply of them! Look it over with us, and then let's
decide what to do."

"You're sure it's safe? He won't catch us?"

"I've got that dray stable in the palm of my sweet little
hand, Agate Eyes. Don't you worry about that! We can't
see into the little room until he goes in there, and we're
able to get into the smithy. Then—"

"How do you get into the smithy?"

Johnny looked pained. "You forget who you're talking
to, or something? I was in there last night, to bore my peepholes. It's mighty hard to keep me out of any old place,
when it's my job to go in."

"Where is Vi?"

"In the stable, with Denny and George Flowers, where
did you think?"

"I don't know if that's very smart, Johnny." Hewitt frowned. "I wish Denny had sent her back here to the hotel, and assigned one of his Secret Service men to keep watch over her."

"You tell her that, Agate Eyes. You're the one made her a full partner."

They returned to the old stable, keeping almost a block apart, Johnny in the lead. When he arrived there, Hewitt was admitted by an alley door before he could knock. He was introduced to Colonel Flowers of the Texas Rangers, a man who could have passed for an elderly shoe clerk or bookkeeper. Not quite portly, dressed in a little more than the height of Texas fashion, he would have been an easy man to underrate. Hewitt did not make that mistake.

Denny was at the peephole. He made way for Hewitt, saying, "He's got a bushel of them sliced off, and he's still going. Don't worry—that saw makes so much noise, he won't hear you."

The locked smithy was dark, but the stable was even darker, and there was no problem of adjusting his eyes to see clearly what went on in the Peerless shop. The first thing that struck Hewitt was the beautiful efficiency of the shop. A small but powerful vertical-boiler steam engine ran a master shaft. Belts from pulleys on the master shaft ran a big bar cutter, a heavy trip hammer and a light one, a swage press for hot-forging, a big grinder with a burnishing brush, two drill presses, and two lathes.

It also ran the high-speed hacksaw, which today had on the narrow, fine-cut blade. The fine-tooth ratchet feed moved the bar of brass stock along the bed for another cut, the moment the saw raised itself after finishing the last cut. The shining blanks dropped in a small basket, and when Hewitt put his eye to the peephole, Kotrzina was standing there with his hands on his hips, watching the basket fill.

The mainshaft also ran a tumbler, a barrel mounted at an angle of about forty-five degrees. Hewitt could not see into it from the peephole, but he knew it would be full of sand. The blanks fresh from the saw would be tumbled in sand for however long it took to remove, by the abrasion of the sand, any rough edges left by the saw. They would come out of the tumbler glittering at their brightest.

Kotrzina had removed his shirt and undershirt, and had a leather apron on to protect his bare torso and pants. As Hewitt watched, he took a sandwich from a box and bit into it, washing it down with beer poured from a pitcher into a tin can. Once he winced and waved a hand, to shake out the pain. He was completely absorbed in what he was doing, so cocksure that he could not conceive of anyone doing anything as stupidly simple as boring a peephole through his wall.

Hewitt felt Vi's hand on his arm and smelled her perfume. He stepped back from the peephole. Johnny was across the room, telling McGucken and Flowers about the ten-gauge shotgun-cannon that protected Kotrzina when he worked in the little secret room.

They joined the three men. "Not so good, is it?" Denny said. "How the dickens do you get past the shotgun?"

"I don't know yet," said Hewitt, "but there has to be a way. Can you have Pikus and Asbury keep watch on him the rest of the afternoon, and until they're relieved this evening?"

"Yes, but I don't know what good it will do, if we have no plan for going in after him."

"Denny, we have several days to work up a plan, if we need that long. He has a lot of blanks cut now, and he's still sawing away. All those blanks have to be stamped on both sides, and the edges milled. Let's get together here tonight, and see what we come up with."

"When? What time?"

"After it's good and dark. Our mutual friend is working hard—for him, anyway—and he has some sore fingers. Let's see if something doesn't come to us tonight, and meanwhile, let him get wearier and his hands more painful."

"I don't like to run something like this on the inspiration of the moment."

"We won't. But neither are we going to pass up any chances that come to us. Get your agents on the job here, and the rest of us will catch some rest. I don't know anyone who deserves it more."

Denny slipped out first to hurry and send either Pikus or Asbury back to stand watch. George Flowers went next, and then Johnny Quillen. He would wait at the end of the alley, to see that Vi got back safely to the hotel. Hewitt was to wait until one of the Secret Service agents relieved him.

The door closed behind Johnny. In the dark, hot stable, Vi turned and faced Hewitt, laying her hand on his arm. "Jeff, I want to ask you to do something for me," she said in a low voice.

"Sure, Vi, anything," he said.

She studied him a moment, her head cocked to one side, a little frown on her lovely face. "I really haven't been a burden, have I? I've been a full partner, haven't I?"

"You haven't been a burden and you are a full partner, and a good one."

"Then I can ask one little-bitty thing, can't I?"

He took her by the arms and whispered, "Can I guess what it is?"

"You better!" she said.

He gathered her into his arms and kissed her, and she went limp against him, and her mouth opened to take his hungry kiss. She disengaged herself from him and stepped back.

"That wasn't so little-bitty, was it?" she said unsteadily. "Jeff, we'd have lovely children, you and I."

"If they took after you, yes."

She looked away. "And what a mother I'd be, for about a year! Then you'd be off to hell and gone somewhere on a case, and I'd come to my senses. I'd hand the baby over to old Maria, on the ranch, and off I'd go, too."

"You would?"

"Yes. So don't let me let you make a fool of yourself, will you? I married one good man and ruined his life. I won't do it to you."

"We'll have to talk this over again, my dear. You don't make such a decision alone, not when I love you as I think I love you."

"Oh yes I do! You're smart, Jeff, but you'll never know me as I know myself. I'll see to that! I love you too, dear, and that's why I won't marry you."

She got through the door before he could catch her, and he watched her run lightly up the alley toward where Johnny Quillen should be waiting. He returned to the peephole in time to see Kotrzina dump a fresh load of blanks into the tumbler and start fishing out polished ones as they came to the top of the sand. Even without direct sunlight in the tightly locked smithy, the polished discs glittered like fire.

CHAPTER ELEVEN

Hewitt and Vi ate together at the Condon House.

"What are you going to do after dinner?" she asked.

"Catch a short nap, and do some thinking," he said.

"May I wait in your room with you? I don't stand solitude very well. If I have to stay locked in my room much longer, they may as well pad the walls. I won't bother you."

"I don't see why not," he said.

"Is that the best you can do?"

He leaned toward her, gave her what he hoped would be interpreted as a look of almost insupportable longing. "In the time available, yes," he said.

"You dog!"

They had agreed to meet at the dray stables at ten, after darkness had fallen. It was heavily overcast, and suffocatingly humid, and there was a real threat of rain. A good hard rain, Hewitt thought, would help. The new office addition at the Peerless works had a flat roof. Hard rain would resound on it like an infantry battle. They would not have to worry about small noises alerting the count.

Denny had reported that Milt Asbury, one of his Secret Service agents, had "summer complaint" and a high fever. He would be out of action. But Hugh Pikus, the other agent, would be there. That would give them a raiding party of five men—Hewitt, Denny, Johnny, Pikus, and George Flowers—plus one woman. It was rather more of a compliment than Hewitt felt like paying Kotrzina; but the count had the others spooked.

They left the table a little after seven, Hewitt helping Vi to her feet tenderly. He made sure his coat was open, his own .45 in the holster he had made himself, clipped inside the waistband of his pants. It would practically fall into his hand in an emergency.

They crossed the crowded dining room toward the lobby, and almost bumped into Count Carl Kotrzina, who was just entering. The count started to close the door behind himself. He recognized them in time, and held it open with a bow.

"Thank you, Kotrzina. Have a nice supper," Hewitt said.

"So nice of you," Kotrzina murmured. "Perhaps we shall soon have that ride on horseback, Viola?"

Hewitt said, "I doubt it. You're going to be up to your noble rump in trouble in a few days. I don't believe I'd plan ahead too far, if I were you."

The count narrowed his eyes slightly. I suppose, Hewitt thought, that's supposed to be a threatening look. . . . "You are insolent, Hewitt," Kotrzina said. "It would be, I think, appropriate to whip you, to punish you."

"Have me whipped, perhaps. You know better than to fool with me, boy!"

Kotrzina pushed past them, with another small bow to Vi. They went into the lobby, Hewitt murmuring, "Man in a hurry to get back to work. Changed his shirt and put on a tie, but he smells of sweat. Vi, tonight we're going to nail him good!"

"He wasn't quite sure how he felt about seeing us together, you know," she replied.

He nodded. "I thought so myself. Likes the idea that you'll be keeping me occupied tonight, so he can work in peace. But hurt that you could prefer anyone to him."

"Yes. Funny thing, Jeff, I'm not afraid of him suddenly. As you say, he's a gutless man living in a dream."

"Glad to realize it, but keep a gun handy."

Vi stopped at the desk to pick up a deck of cards. "Mr. Hewitt and I are going upstairs now," she told the clerk. "Mr. Kotrzina will probably come into the lobby, the moment we're at the head of the stairs to see where we go. As soon as he has gone back into the dining room, will you send someone to Mr. Hewitt's room to let us know?"

The clerk agreed. They climbed the wide stairs, and turned into Hewitt's room. Not two minutes later, the clerk himself knocked at the door. "You were right, Mrs. Chaney," he reported. "As soon as he saw you go in, he went back into the dining room."

Hewitt kicked off his boots and lay down on his back on the bed. Vi spread out a game of solitaire on the desk. "You couldn't do what I did there," she said.

"What's that?"

"Ask the clerk to spy for you. He'd be offended. But he'll do it for a Dempsey and a Chaney."

"I don't doubt that a bit."

"The count has been thrown in the shade, did you know that? We have royalty in Austin for a few days."

"Oh, who?"

"A son of the Gaekwar of Baroda. He's inspecting the construction of the new capitol. Baroda is one of the richest provinces in India, and the Gaekwar is its emperor, or sultan."

"I'm not exactly unlearned, Madame la Chaney."

"Poor Jeff! You want to sleep, don't you?"

He said nothing, and she remained quiet. He never did really fall asleep, but he did drift into that state where he both rested and refreshed his body, and did some of his best thinking. He was never nervous, closing in on a man to bring a case to an end, but neither did he like to leave anything to chance. He had trained himself to review a job as objectively as he could, going back over it to make sure he had overlooked nothing.

Hewitt knew, without undue self-approbation, that there was no better investigator in the business than himself. It was not genius, and he knew that too. He had two qualities that made him pre-eminent. One was willingness to attend to detail, both in action and appraisal. The other was a memory that was naturally absorbent and retentive, and which he had consciously trained to be better still.

He felt that he knew Carl Kotrzina, count of Kothen, Apolda and Cybinka, better than the count knew himself. How right he was could mean thousands of dollars difference in the fees they would collect. If he was wrong, this could be a very lean case indeed.

He sat up, slipped his feet into his boots, and yawned. "Mind if I smoke?" he said.

"Not at all." Vi bunched her cards and began to shuffle them. "We still have more than an hour. Why don't you go get us some coffee, and let's play pinochle?"

"The coffee sounds fine, but the last time I played pinochle, one of the players turned up dead. That's how I got into this case in the first place."

She shivered. "Go get the coffee, and we'll make it pitch."

He was lucky enough to catch a bellboy in the hall, and sent him for coffee. They locked the door behind him, and Vi dealt the cards with the nimble skill with which she did everything.

"That Peerless place is in kind of a Mexican part of town, isn't it?" he asked her.

"Yes, why?"

"Know where I can buy a *piñata* there? Pick it up on the way, and save me a trip tomorrow."

"Jeff, are you sure you know what you're talking about? A *piñata* is a child's birthday thing, a clay pot with a papier-mâché form over it, a rooster or bull or dragon or something. You fill it with candy and the kids—"

"I know what a *piñata* is, but I don't know where to buy one and I need one, and instead of telling me where I can buy one, you want to lecture me."

She slammed a trump five down on his king lead, and led back the trump king. "High, low and jack," she said, "and I'll buy your damned *piñata* for you, but I wish to heaven you would keep your mind on your work. Count Kotrzina is our *piñata,* and we ought to be thinking about cracking him."

"I have been. Make you a little bet, sugar."

"What?"

"We're going to be one man short on our raiding party tonight."

She frowned. "How do you figure that?"

"Deal the cards," he said, "and think it over. You know as much about this as I do. Do you mean to say it hasn't occurred to you that we're going to be one man short?"

She dealt the cards. He bid three. She thought it over, and passed. From his four hearts, he led his trey for low. She smiled malevolently as she dropped the deuce on it. He made high, jack and game, tying the score.

"All right, you insufferable *macho* monster, what am I overlooking that should tell me that we'll be a man short on our raiding party?" she said.

He showed her all his teeth in a smile. "Honey, if you were the governor of Texas, commanding one of the most famous police agencies in the world, and one of the richest

Oriental princes in the world visited your capital, where would you have the superintendent of that justly famous force of Texas Rangers? Guarding the Gaekwar, in full dress uniform, or helping a crew of two-bit detectives pull in a penny-ante chicken-thief like Kotrzina?"

She thought it over. "You're right. Does it bother you that we have to go in without George Flowers?"

"It delights me."

"It delights you?" she cried. "Why?"

"I can handle Denny and Johnny. I think I can handle you. But nobody can handle that old diamondback Ranger. Be patient, my dear. Eventually, you'll see what I mean."

"Oh, how I hate you!"

"There's one thing you have to do for me. Once we pull this raid off—"

"*If* we pull it off."

"We will. I don't quite know how we're going to deal with his cannon, but we'll deal with it, never fear. And when we've got him in cuffs, Denny McGucken is going to be a very busy Treasury man. He'll want to take custody of the prisoner himself, and he'll want the dies, the blanks, the half-finished coins, and all the other evidence. He has only one man to help him.

"I don't want him to see me whispering to Johnny, so I want you to get to Johnny, and *see that he volunteers to help Denny!* Once Denny agrees to that, the question of who will guard the premises is going to come up. If it doesn't, you bring it up and nominate me.

"I'll probably be there most of the night. I want you to see to it that George Flowers gets the word, after we have pulled off the raid. But I want at least a couple of hours there alone, before Flowers relieves me. I know I can count on you to handle that."

She pointed her finger at him. "You don't miss a trick, do you? Jeff, you're wonderful!"

"At least that," he said modestly.

She took him confidently through the dark town, holding his left arm with her right hand. In a few minutes after leaving the hotel, they were in a district as Mexican as Matamoros. The sounds, the smells, the very feeling of time, were all different.

They stopped at a little *tienda,* where Vi asked about a *piñata.* Hewitt noted, with satisfaction, that her Spanish was not Texas Spanish. It was better than his, and better than that spoken by most border Mexicans. The merchant sent them around the corner to another place, where again they were redirected. Everyone seemed to know Vi, and they talked to her without the polite reserve that most Anglos received in this area.

They found a man who had a whole storage room full of *piñatas.* Hewitt selected a *grandote*—a big one—and did a little chaffering over the price, rather than raise suspicion. It was a burro of pink and green paper, with big lavender eyes.

He let Vi lead the way, now, and he followed, swinging the *piñata* in his left hand. He kept his right close to his belly and his .45. *His Nibs is surely working, and if he isn't, we're up the flue tonight for sure,* he thought. *But somehow I just don't trust him worth a damn. . . .*

They reached the dray stable, and Vi tapped softly on the door. Johnny Quillen opened it and let them in. Hewitt felt better the moment he was through the door, and could hear the rhythmic *tump-tump-tump* from the Peerless works. That could be only a high-speed die press, and it meant that the count was at work.

"Everybody here but Colonel Flowers," Johnny said.

"Don't count on him. Royalty in town, and he's got the duty, I'm sure," Hewitt said.

It began to rain then, softly at first, but harder quickly. Soon it was a steady, hard drumming that resonated loudly through the stable. It took a moment for Hewitt's eyes to get used to the darkness. He saw Denny McGucken and Pikus across the room talking together.

"We may be up against it, Agate Eyes," Johnny said, leading Hewitt over to where the Treasury men stood. "We already been in the shop and had a look at his shop. He's making coins, all right. But that goddamn place is a fortress, and Denny and me just about decided that the only way we're going to get him out is set fire to the roof. Now, with this goddamn rain, we can't even do that."

Denny took Hewitt by the arm. "Come on, I'll show you how to get into the shop. You're going to get a little wet, but there's no help for it. One at a time."

"I'll take Mrs. Chaney in with me," Hewitt said.

"I don't think I like that. The more people there are, the more chance of somebody falling or knocking something down. We don't want to notify him that we're here."

"I'll still take her in with me. Denny, this is the trade I work at! Do you want to instruct me in it?"

"No, but—"

"Everybody should go in. We're going to have to kick in the office door from inside the shop, aren't we?"

"No, it's locked, but Johnny has a key that fits it. It's when we get into the office that the trouble begins. That damned shotgun is vise-mounted, and the rope that pulls both triggers is about three inches from his head, as he sits at the press."

"Why not just whistle through the peephole, and tell him he's under arrest, Denny? If we're locked out, he's locked in. So is the evidence. Where is he going to go?"

Denny said passionately, "Jefferson, I want to lay hands on this man. I want him alive, and he's the kind who could commit suicide. I want the evidence, above all, those dies. He has made such asses of us, and the Secretary is so desperately anxious that I have nightmares about it."

"You're afraid he's that much smarter than you are?"

"I *know* he is that much smarter than I. This is the most brilliant criminal genius the world has ever seen."

No use arguing with him, and for the time being, it suited Hewitt that Denny should be so distraught. He said, "I don't think Flowers will be here. He'll be guarding some visiting royalty. We're going to have to do it ourselves."

"Oh, my stars, no!"

Hewitt patted him on the back. "Don't worry, we'll make out, but we need all hands on deck in the smithy. You lead the way, and we'll follow."

They had entered the stable by the alley door, but Denny now led them out into the street. The door to the Peerless works was only a few feet away, and he had left it unlocked. He ducked inside, followed by Vi, with Hewitt a step behind. Then came Hugh Pikus, and last of all, Johnny Quillen, who locked the door behind them.

"Nice, quiet door. Your work, Johnny?" said Hewitt.

"Sure. First thing I do when I go in like this is make sure the hinges and locks don't squeak." He pointed. "Yander, behind the hacksaw. He's got two lamps in there, and one of them is right in front of the hole, almost. Be sure you look down, or you'll be blind."

The little window of brass filings under the big power hacksaw glittered even in the dark. The efficient little steam engine was silent, but the boiler sighed under a full head of steam, and a hot coke fire glowed in the grates. The steam pipe from the boiler led through the wall near the ground, almost under Johnny's peephole. Except for this steam line, which would have puzzled an outsider, it was one of the best-looking machine shops Hewitt had ever seen—the machine tools all new, shafting, pulleys and belts new too, and everything swept and dusted spotlessly. The tool carriers and chucks on both lathes had dust covers, and there was a glass safety screen over the emery wheel of the big grinder.

Very good workman, this nobleman. . . . When Hewitt put the flat of his hand against the wall, he could feel as well as hear the hard, regular vibration of the die press. He took off his hat and applied an eye to the peephole, directing his vision downward as he had been warned. Some of the old, familiar excitement slithered through him, as he felt himself closing in, once more, on a man with a big reward on him. Nothing like money to make a chase interesting!

It was a snug little den that Kotrzina had for himself; the word "fortress" was not inappropriate at all. The first thing Hewitt saw was the ten-gauge, double-barreled shotgun behind Kotrzina, its sawed-off barrels pointed at the only door into the room. It was clamped into a stout vise, with both triggers attached to an efficient little trip that was activated by a light rope. The rope ran up to the ceiling, through a pulley, and across the ceiling to another pulley. From there, it dangled within easy reach of Kotrzina's hands.

The press was run by silent gears turned by a small but obviously powerful steam turbine, a gray-painted, cast-steel snail half as tall as a man. The turbine also powered, through a shaft, pulley, and belt, another small burnishing wheel beside the press.

It was not a small press, either. Hewitt had conceived something more portable in his mind—something that would require a special brass alloy, probably softened by the addition of some lead. Not so. This one was perfectly capable of making a good, sharp impression in pure brass, perhaps even in soft iron.

The head holding the die rose only about an inch and a half. It was directed in its movement by an eccentric cam that brought it down fast and hard, and then applied a second or two of maximum pressure before raising it again. As best Hewitt could time it, the press was turning out an impression about every two seconds.

Only one side of the coin was being struck, however, and the edges remained smooth. The coins would have to be fed through the press again, to imprint the other side, and still again, to cut the milling on the edges. Then, of course, they would have to be burnished to remove any tiny shreds of metal, either at the steel-wire brush of the burnishing wheel, or in the sand-filled tumbler in the smithy.

Across the room was a stout sink made of two-inch Louisiana cypress, the electroplating vat where, so far at least, Kotrzina had coated his coins with an infinitesimal skin of real gold. On a shelf above the sink stood two big glass jugs, or carboys, holding five gallons of etching acid each. Under the sink stood row on row of galvanic batteries, to supply the electric current for plating.

Kotrzina sat in profile in the middle of his little private mint, hunched over his high-speed die press, feeding blanks into the chuck with the thumb and finger of his right hand, and removing stamped pieces with the thumb and finger of his left. He had stripped to the waist again, and his body glistened with sweat. He was completely absorbed in his work—and he had to be, because the fingers of both hands were stiff and swollen.

Every two seconds, he delicately but swiftly picked up a stamped piece with his left hand. Slipped a fresh blank in with his right, just before the die came down. Out with the impressed piece, in with another blank. Out, in. Out, in—thirty coins a minute.

Hewitt stepped back from the peephole and motioned Vi to take his place. She watched a long time, and then moved back with Hewitt to join the men in the center of the dark, shadowy shop.

"Got any ideas, Agate Eyes?" said Johnny.

"Sure! It's a waltz. But I do have to remind you that it was my town drunk who tipped us about the shotgun. I'd be mopping you boys up with a handful of old undershirts, if you had kicked that door in."

"Rub it in, Hewitt," McGucken snapped, "but damn it, man, this is no time to joke. I've got to take that man alive. I've got to do a clean job on which the Secretary can report to the President with pride. You say it's a waltz. I hope you're not bragging or bluffing."

"I'm not. Cool down, Dennis, me boy!" Hewitt looked at Vi, and put a hand on her shoulder. "Can you shoot that thirty-eight of yours through that peephole and hit anything? Will the lamp blind you?"

"There's no way you could hit Carl, lamp or no lamp, and I wouldn't shoot a man in the back anyway," she said.

"You won't be shooting at him. All you have to do is hit one of those carboys of acid on the shelf across the room. His hands are already in bad shape. When five gallons of acid shower out over the room, just as that press is banging down, I think he'll muff something. I think it's a hundred to one that he'll mangle a hand."

Johnny whistled softly. "Can't miss, can't miss! Those coins are only about three thirty-seconds of an inch thick. Christ, what that would do to your hand!"

Denny took hold of Hewitt's arm in the dark. "How do

we time it? Come on, man, once we've got him maimed, how do we handle him?"

"We'll go into the office with a sledge hammer. The minute Vi fires, I smash the lock and we go in before he knows what's happening. First thing we do is disarm the shotgun. Best way to do that is grab the hammers, palm down. I'll do that. The rest of you help yourselves."

"Fine," said Johnny, taking off his coat, "but I'll swing the sledge hammer. I cut my teeth on one of them."

"Vi, take a look and tell us if you can hit one of those carboys."

She peered through the hole, and then looked back at him. "I could hit a dime pasted to either one of them."

"Just hit one of the jugs, low enough to release a lot of flying acid—that's all we ask of you. Wait until we tell you we're ready, and then good luck."

Johnny selected a hammer. They unlocked the office with his skeleton key, and went inside. Johnny calmly lighted a hanging lamp, and then moved a chair and desk out of the way. He spat on both hands, rubbed them together, and picked up the heavy hammer as though it were a fly swatter.

"Ready when you are," he said.

"I'll go first to grab the shotgun. As far as I'm concerned, Denny, you can tell Vi to go ahead."

Denny leaned out of the office door, framed by the lamplight, and waved his arm.

CHAPTER TWELVE

Johnny took a chance and swung the hammer as Denny made his signal. It was too risky, but he got away with it. They heard the blast of the .38, sounding like a cannon in the closed shop, and the deep, hoarse screaming of a man in agony, just as the lock broke and the door flew open.

Hewitt had the shotgun in two steps, but he need not have worried about it. Kotrzina had half risen from his chair and was clutching the little table of the press with his left hand. Every muscle was locked rock-tight and hard, and he went on screaming and staring at his mangled right hand.

The blood was spurting from it. Hewitt lowered the hammers of the shotgun and detached the trigger rope. He yanked out his handkerchief and jumped to help Kotrzina stop the loss of blood. Kotrzina saw him and turned and struck at him with both hands, smearing him with blood. He knocked Hewitt backward to the floor and dropped on him, trying to get hold of him with his teeth.

"Stop it, you damned fool, I'm trying to help you!" Hewitt shouted.

It was no good. He got his knees up in time to protect his crotch from Kotrzina's knee. Kotrzina dived at him and sank his teeth in Hewitt's left biceps. Hewitt twisted on his left side and snaked the sap out of his pocket, but he could not get a swing with it.

The horrible thing was that Kotrzina seemed to be insensitive to the pain in his hand. His sweat-slippery body gave Johnny, Denny, and Pikus no grip. The Secret Service man got hold of Kotrzina's belt, but there was no way to stop those flailing, bloody hands and no way to free that bulldog grip the man had with his teeth.

Someone grabbed the sap from Hewitt's hand. He saw the swift arc it cut through the air. Kotrzina went limp. Vi said, dangling the sap in her hand, "That's right, all you men get excited and let him kill Jeff." She was magnificently calm.

The pain in Hewitt's left arm, where Kotrzina had bitten him, was excruciating, but he helped stanch the flow of blood from the counterfeiter's ruined hand. Pikus seemed to have more than ordinary knowledge of first aid. He found a pressure point that he could hold with his fingertip until he had bound up the hand. By then, Kotrzina was stirring, licking his lips, and making weak puppy noises in his throat.

"He'll lose his three largest fingers, but if we get him to the doctor in a hurry, he'll still have the small one and the thumb," said Pikus, as he snapped his handcuffs on the man. "Where's the nearest doctor?"

Vi looked at Johnny. "Get Lowell," she said, and Johnny nodded and trotted off through the rain. Hewitt thought, she comes through in a pinch. She has a right to take charge, and yet—a woman that good with a sap? It's something to think about. . . .

Kotrzina became conscious, but all the fight was gone out of him. Vi stood guard over him, the sap at the ready, while Hewitt showed Denny how to remove the die from the press. Denny sent Pikus to bring containers for the die, the blanks, and the coins that had already been struck on one side. He searched in vain for the other two dies—the one to strike the reverse side of the coin, and the one to cut the milling marks on the edges.

"He should have a lot of good money somewhere, too," Denny grumbled. "Tomorrow, we'll go through this whole shop and his house. We'll tear it to pieces, board by board, if we have to."

"If a human being hid it," Hewitt comforted him, "a human being can find it."

"I'm not so sure he's human," said Denny. "Well, one thing at a time."

Hewitt tried to talk to Kotrzina. He was sure the man heard and understood him, but he doubted that he could discipline his brain and body to reply. The count, with only a mangled hand, reminded him of men he had seen who had been mortally wounded by a heavy .45 slug. It was as though something had exploded in him, so that the entire body was one great, quivering wound. He wondered if Kotrzina would ever think and talk and feel, as a human being thinks and talks and feels, again.

It had stopped raining by the time Johnny and Dr. Chaney got there. The doctor wanted the count carried to his house as swiftly as possible for surgery. He looked at Hewitt's wounded biceps, shaking his head.

"You could have a bad arm out of this. There's no laceration, but there is considerable destruction of tissue. I've seen gangrene result from wounds like that. We'll want to keep a careful watch on it."

"The best thing, it seems to me, is to keep using it as much as I can," said Hewitt.

"Right, keep the blood circulating around it, but it will hurt."

"It hurts anyway. I'm not going to sleep tonight, so I'll stay here and guard the place until morning. I'll have a chance to look around for the missing evidence and keep my game arm moving at the same time."

"Sure you feel up to it, Jefferson?" McGucken said. And thus was disposed of the problem of how Hewitt would manage to stay in the shop alone tonight.

Kotrzina had to be carried out. He was shivering so violently that the weakness could not have been simulated; nevertheless, Denny removed his shoes and chained his feet together first. Vi looked longingly at Hewitt, but he shook his head, and she went out behind the doctor. He went to the street door of the Peerless works with them, closed it behind them, and shot the big oak bar through the heavy iron loops.

Thanks to the fortress-like construction the count had lavished on the place, he would not be bothered now. Several hurricane lanterns hung in the machine shop. As he went about lighting them, the steam boiler's safety pop-off valve blew, venting a tall plume of white vapor through the escape in the roof.

He checked the coke-burning boiler. Kotrzina had a bed of coals here that would have lasted all night. Once the die press was shut down and the drain of steam ceased, pressure had built up quickly. He opened the injector and pulled cold water into the boiler, and banked the fire with a scattering of sand. It would turn to slag quickly, and the fireman would call him bad names tomorrow, but it did the job. The pop-off valve closed.

He spent an hour and a half in what was a swift but superficial search. He had to break open Kotrzina's desk. He found three prepaid orders from an alloy foundry in Philadelphia that surely would be enough to convict the count. The materials ordered were listed only by stock number, but the foundry's stock list would inevitably show that number to identify cylindrical brass.

How brilliant the man was in so many ways, and yet how stupid to leave these incriminating papers in his own desk! But this was primarily of interest to the Treasury Department. Hewitt was looking for something else, and sniffing around like a bird dog was not going to find it for him. He sat down and tried to forget the pain in his arm in the chair Kotrzina had occupied at the die press. He deliberately stopped wrestling with his problem, and let his mind drift.

Someone was pounding on the street door, not loudly but insistently. He went to answer it, knowing who it would be, and not very happy about it. She came in, carrying a stone jug of hot coffee and a bag of sandwiches. He merely nodded to her as he admitted her, and she saw the look on his face and did not speak.

She followed him into the little shop behind the office, and handed him a sandwich. He took it and sat down again in Kotrzina's chair at the die press. In a moment, she handed him the coffee jug. He drank from it and handed it back. He saw her tip it up expertly and drink too.

"This is where it is," he said harshly. "He wouldn't leave it where anyone else could get close to it."

He was grateful that she did not speak. Handy she might be with a gun and sap, but she was a comfortable creature to have around. He held his sandwich in his left hand and dropped his right on the valve that fed steam to the turbine. He opened it slightly, heard the musical whine as it started turning.

He threw the press in gear and watched it work. He had always liked fine machinery, yet had never had the time or opportunity to develop the talents he thought he had for it. He and Conrad had often talked of financing a machine shop in Cheyenne, but had decided the time was not ripe for it. Of course they would never think of investing as much as the count had in this superb German equipment; for one thing, they would not have his easy access to money.

Slowly, he opened the steam valve wider and wider. Thus the count had developed his skill in feeding the blanks into the machine, starting slowly and increasing its speed as his dexterity increased. With some sort of automatic feed, this press was good enough to strike a hundred coins a minute. No doubt that would have been Kotrzina's next investment, once he—

The turbine began chattering with vibration, and he closed the valve swiftly. The high howl died to a low growl, and then it was silent altogether. He reached for the coffee jug with his good arm, and grinned at Vi as she handed it to him.

"What's funny?" she asked.

"Why," he said, "would a man spend so much money on fine machine tools and so much time installing them secretly himself, and then leave a high-speed steam turbine to knock itself to pieces if it's run faster than at half speed?"

"I have no idea, but I'm sure you do."

"Right again, and the prize goes to the lady with the buck teeth and knock knees in the third row! Look, Vi, I'm going to stick my neck under the ax, and you can chop away if I turn out to be wrong. Look at the massive concrete and masonry base under that turbine! Big enough for one twice as big, believe me," he said jovially, forgetting the pain in his arm in his excitement.

"But then he mounted it on steel bolts set in the masonry —*without lock nuts!* I'm not a machinist, but I've got sense enough to know that a turbine that turns eight or ten thousand revolutions a minute is going to transmit intense vibrations to those bolts. The only way you can keep the nuts from working loose is to lock them down with another set of nuts, turned down tight.

"Only, this turbine would run only at half speed on this job load, and lock nuts would slow him down if he ever had to dismount the turbine in a hurry. Look in the corner, there—a big end wrench, a couple of crowbars, a pipe wrench. Nothing there to make anyone suspicious, is there? Just what you'd expect in a good machine shop. Only—why here? Why not outside in the shop?"

She nodded, her eyes bright with excitement, but she did not waste words to say that she understood. She followed him and held the lantern while he turned off the steam at the boiler. They returned to the little shop behind the office. He used the pipe wrench to crack a joint in the line, and release the remaining pressure.

With the heavy end wrench, he removed the nuts of the steel bolts that held the turbine to the massive concrete base. He drove one of the big bars under the turbine and pried up, and without being told, Vi knelt and slipped one of the wood shims that were inconspicuously stacked against the wall under it.

They went around to the other side of the turbine and repeated the process. A little at a time, they raised the mass of steel until it stood on level blocks of wood, above the bolts and free of them.

Using the bar slowly, almost tenderly, he began edging it sidewise, Vi inserting more wood shims under it as it moved. He had to shift it a good three inches before the square hole in the base appeared, and two more before he could see into it. Vi held the lantern while he inserted his hand and groped for the bottom.

He had to thrust his hand between stack after stack of bundled currency to find the cold concrete bottom, and the canvas bag of gold coins that was under everything. He let Vi put her hand in, and take out four or five of the bundles. The money was in businesslike bales of one hundred pieces each.

Her eyes sparkled, and her face glowed pinkly with animation. "You know what, Jeff? I bet we're going to need another *piñata,"* she said.

"You're pretty smart, aren't you?" he said. "Think you could find one, this time of night, and someone who'll come by in about an hour and take them to the hotel?"

"I'm on my way." She got to her feet.

"Vi, are you sure you'll be safe?"

"I'm one person who would be safe anywhere in Austin," she replied.

He let her out the street door, locked it behind her, and counted money while she was gone. He had entirely forgotten that he had a bad arm. He did not have to count the gold pieces. The bag had a label in the count's tiny, neat handwriting, $5,000 eagles, $10,000 double eagles. He had only to untie it and verify what he knew already, that it was all good American coinage.

By the time Vi got back with the other *piñata,* a gaudy rooster, he had counted $65,000 in currency and had it neatly stacked in two piles. "Mr. Escobedo will be around in an hour," Vi said. "You mean you're going to send him to the hotel with all this money? Alone?"

"Not all of it. We're going to leave all the gold, and—oh, say about four thousand in currency, here. Treasury has to recover something, don't they? And there has to be ten thousand here that I can claim for Si Taylor."

"Suppose Treasury doesn't want to settle with him?"

"Then Treasury can whistle for the only big supply of the count's finished coins. Denny doesn't even know who has them, but I told him they exist. Don't worry, Vi, he'll have to wire the Secretary for permission to close the deal —but they'll deal," he said.

"The Samaritan Committee will want its ten thousand back, and we're going to leave them almost enough for that—almost, but not quite. Treasury is going to have to levy on the shop for the balance. The rest of it goes to Johnny's client in New York, Great Coast Bank and Trust Company."

"Because they pay fifty per cent reward."

"Exactly! And we don't have to go through the Treasury Department to collect."

"And how do you get it back to them? Johnny takes it?"

"Yes. While your friend, Escobedo, is carrying the *piñatas* to the hotel, you'll stir Johnny out, and he'll notify Denny that we have found the loot. They'll come here at a hard gallop, and I'll be in great pain from my arm. We'll leave them in charge of the money, and you'll go with me to the hotel. We'll store the money in your room, not mine, and you'll stay with me, keeping cold compresses on my sore arm, until Denny has had time to put two and two together.

"He's not a fool, Vi, and I'm afraid he knows me as well as I know him. He's going to show up at the hotel, demanding to see the *piñata* I had here. After he has time to think it over, he's going to realize that he has enough to make the Secretary happy. But at first, it's going to gravel him to realize that we got away with something, and he doesn't know how much or how. In this business, you have to tailor your methods to the people you're dealing with, and Denny's an old cop himself."

"Suspicious, you mean. Like you."

"Like me."

She looked away. "Damn such a business! I like to think I'm sophisticated and hard, but I guess I like people too much to ever want to be that way."

He patted her hand. "The Missouri Pacific will never know the difference, my dear. After this case, they'll call you every time they've got a touchy case."

At seven-thirty, Vi sat at his bedside, heartily enjoying a breakfast of steak and eggs. His own breakfast—a soft-boiled egg, toast and tea—was untouched on the tray. He had sipped a little coffee from her cup, but he wanted Denny to see him going without food.

It was not just Denny, but both Secret Service men too, who knocked at his door. Vi got up, carrying her napkin, and opened the door. "Sh-h! I think he's finally sleeping," she said. "I couldn't get him to eat."

He did not turn over. "I'm not sleeping and I don't want to eat. I just want you to get that damned doctor over here with some painkiller pills."

Denny hesitated, but not long. "This shouldn't take long, Jefferson. In any case, it's my duty."

Hewitt rolled over and snarled, "And you always were a fiend for duty, weren't you? What now?"

Without waiting to be asked, Denny pulled a chair up beside the bed. "Where's that *piñata* you had last night?"

"Down at the desk, I guess. There's two of them, a burro and a rooster. What do you—?"

"No, I brought them up," Vi cut in. "They're in the closet, there."

Denny nodded to the Secret Service men, who went to the closet and brought the *piñatas*. Denny examined them carefully. "You only had one last night," he said.

Hewitt only glared. Vi said, "Mr. Escobedo had to find the rooster. When he brought it, Jeff had him bring them both to the hotel."

"Who is Mr. Escobedo?"

"He runs a store, the Tienda Luz de la Luna, and—"

"He carried those two things here last night, all by himself?"

"Why not?" she cried. "I've know him since I was a little girl. I don't know how it concerns you."

McGucken ignored her and said to Hewitt, "That's a hell of a big hole you found under that steam turbine, and not a lot of money in it."

"Eighteen thousand, seven hundred dollars," Hewitt said. "That's pretty good money to me."

"You know what I mean, Jefferson."

"I know that ten thousand of it goes to a client of ours, and we don't wait for any court order, either."

McGucken put his hands on his hips. "Wait one minute, my friend. The United States Treasury has custody of that money. If you have a client with a claim, he can file it, and it will be given due consideration."

Hewitt sat up painfully—oh, so painfully! "Fine, and you can file a claim for one thousand finished gold slicks. All you have to do is find out who bought them for ten thousand of those dollars you're holding. You saw the way Kotrzina kept books. You'll never know who has them, and if they go into circulation in a year or two, you'll never know where they came from. I don't feel well, Denny, and I want you to finish your business and get the hell out of here. Now what else is on your mind?"

"Jefferson, you can't possibly expect to take ten thousand of that money and hand it over to a client. Why, the Secretary would be outraged if I suggested it."

"He'll be outraged if he doesn't lay hand on those slicks, too."

"I want you to consider your own legal position carefully, Jefferson. Speaking as your friend, it's an indictable offense if you deliberately withhold knowledge of a crime, and this is a serious one. You could—"

"Indict me. Just get out of here, Denny, and let me try to sleep. Indict Johnny, too. Indict Vi while you're at it. Indict Mr. Escobedo. Goddamn it, Johnny and Vi and I broke your case for you, after your Treasury gumshoes fumbled it. We even turned up nineteen thousand dollars in—"

"Eighteen thousand, seven hundred. And, Jeff, the Samaritan Committee has first claim. That's a moral obligation that the Secretary is bound to honor."

"You've got most of it in cash, after my client gets his ten thousand. You've got a blacksmith shop and machine works that must be worth thirty or forty thousand. That's not my problem, Denny, but here's what is: If that damned doctor will ever get here, and give me some pills so I can go to sleep, tomorrow I'm catching a train out of here. If I've got ten thousand in cash on me, I'll come back the next day with fifty thousand in counterfeit. And the way I feel now, I'd just as soon spend the next three days in bed, and let you and the Secretary close it out."

He lay down again. McGucken stood up. "But have you any explanation at all for those *piñatas?*"

"They don't have them in Cheyenne. When I close a case, I go home, where I have friends. Real friends, Denny, not pompous government lawyers."

McGucken patted his arm, taking care to pat the healthy one. "Sorry, old boy. I suppose you're inflexible about your client. As usual! All I can do is wire the Secretary. Better get some rest."

He nodded farewell to Vi, and turned to go with the two Secret Service agents. At the door, he paused and said peevishly, "You had only one *piñata* when you arrived last night. If that hole was full, one wouldn't begin to hold the money. Now you have two. You can't blame me for being suspicious, Jefferson."

Hewitt whirled and reached for the gay red, yellow, and green rooster *piñata,* that Denny had left beside the bed after examining it. He threw it at Denny with all his strength. The Treasury man ducked. The *piñata* crashed against the edge of the door and shattered, pieces of the clay pot showering over the room.

"Now there's only one. Does that satisfy you, or do you want candy and oranges in it, too?" Hewitt said.

Denny shook a fist at him. "You don't fool me one bit, Jefferson, but I'm defeated, and I'll do my best with the Secretary," he said; and went out of the room.

Vi closed the door behind him. Hewitt sat up. "For the love of Mike, get me something to eat," he said.

But his arm was too painfully stiff and sore for him to take the train to San Antonio the next day. Vi made the trip for him, carrying the $10,000 in a small valise that never left her side. He was not at all surprised to learn that she had known Si Taylor since she was a little girl, or that his worthless son, Tommie, had been her first childhood crush.

She returned three days later, with one thousand counterfeit gold pieces. Denny McGucken received them so joyfully that they could be sure that the Secretary bore them no malice over the deal. That same day, Johnny Quillen quietly slipped out of town, carrying $61,300 in currency, destination New York. The Santa Fe had cheerfully agreed to the trip, on company time, when he disclosed that he was returning money that the Great Coast Bank and Trust Company had long ago written off as lost.

That evening, Hewitt left for Brownsville. Vi went with him. There was not much he could do about it, nor was he sure he wanted to. The written, initialed agreement with Lawrence Makenroy was only as good as both parties wanted to make it, and he did not trust the banker. If Vi, in whose childhood home Makenroy had been a guest, could help persuade him that he owed it to his good name to pay up, so much the better. If not, he would enjoy having her there to see him collect anyway.

CHAPTER THIRTEEN

Brownsville was full of rowdy cowboys and cavalrymen.
Two herds were being held on the outskirts of town, and
buyers were choosing animals for shipment to England.
Some of the best had to be discarded for lack of horns.
There were no wharves here, and cattle had to be swum out
to the ship and roped. They were hoisted on board by a
crane, with a rope around their horns, Vi said.

Hewitt would have gone straight across the border to
see Makenroy, but Vi wanted to freshen up first. They had
ridden in silence most of the way, she with her arm through
his and her feet up on the next seat, like him. She had slept
soundly for several hours, with her head on his shoulder.
He had gone sleepless.

He took her out to Mrs. Frank's place, and engaged two
rooms. Buzz Barron was painting industriously. While Mrs.
Frank and Vi went inside, Hewitt talked to Barron.

"How long did Makenroy stay here, Buzz?"

"Until this morning. He got a telegram pretty early, and
woke me up to hitch up a horse and take him home. Would
it help you any to know what that telegram said?"

"It might."

Barron handed it to him. "He had a cat-fit, he did, when
he found he'd lost the blamed thing. I didn't find it until I
got back here."

"I'll bet," said Hewitt. He read:

KOTRZINA JAILED FEDERAL COUNTERFEITING
CHARGES STOP GRAND JURY TO BE IMPANELED
WILL ALSO CONSIDER MURDER CHARGES STOP MY
BEST INFORMATION HE FINISHED STOP WE NOT
INVOLVED HOPE YOU SAME URGE PROTECT SELF

                                        GLOVER

Jesse Glover was an Austin banker. How these types did
stick together! "I'll probably see Makenroy today. Want
me to give him this?" Hewitt said.

"It'd probably be a favor to him," said Buzz.

"I'll bet," Hewitt said for the second time.

Buzz went to get Mrs. Frank's team out. He hitched
them to the buggy and held them until Vi came out, looking
more feminine than Hewitt had ever seen her. She wore a
pale pink peek-a-boo waist, under it an elaborate picot
camisole. Her lightweight skirt was cut full, and the little
"modesty weights" sewn into the hem made it swirl intoxi-
catingly when she turned suddenly. She turned suddenly
fairly often.

An hour later, they pulled up in front of Lawrence
Makenroy's house in Matamoros. A *mozo* came out to lead
the team into the shade, and hold it until it was wanted
again. The same shy little maid opened the door at their
knock. The señor, she said, was not at home.

Hewitt spoke to her in Spanish. "I think he is. Tell him—
or tell someone—that Señora Chaney is with me. Be a good
girl, and just carry that message, will you?"

She had them step inside and wait. She vanished back
into the house, and in a moment, Makenroy came hurrying out. He ignored Hewitt except for a curt nod, to take
both of Vi's hands.

"My dear child, what a delightful surprise! How long

since I've seen you? My word, you grow younger and more lovely every day," he said.

She gave him a prim cheek to kiss, but freed her hands. "Mr. Hewitt and I are partners, Lawrence. We want to talk business with you."

He gave Hewitt a cold, short glance from rather bloodshot eyes. "I can't imagine what about, but please come into my office. Best place to talk business, eh?"

He took Vi by the arm, with suffocating solicitude, and let Hewitt do the best he could. It was Hewitt who closed the door behind them. Makenroy helped Vi to a chair. Hewitt took one near the desk without waiting to be asked. Makenroy went behind the desk, but did not sit down. He opened a desk drawer and took out a long cigar, a planter's crook, but did not immediately light it. Hewitt was sure he had opened the drawer to reassure himself that his gun was there. He smiled a little bleakly at Vi.

"What is it, child? I'm rather a busy man you know. How may I help you?"

"Mr. Hewitt will explain," Vi said. She gave him her sweetest smile.

Makenroy condescended to look at Hewitt. "What did you wish to discuss with me?"

"Not a damn thing. We came here to pick up fifteen thousand dollars, under the terms of this," Hewitt said. He tossed the copy of the agreement he and Makenroy had initialed on the desk.

Makenroy unfolded it enough to look at it, without picking it up. "Rubbish. If this is all you have to discuss, I shan't detain you any longer."

"We don't want to be detained. We just want our money."

"On that? You extorted that out of me almost at gunpoint. It can't possibly be considered a binding agreement by any reasonable person."

There was a short, wide knife with a stiff, thick blade on the desk. Hewitt leaned forward to pick it up. He hefted it in his palm, with his eyes closed, and confirmed what he already knew. It was weighted to be thrown by the tip, not from flat on the palm. Gypsy style, European style, rather than Mexican or Cuban.

He looked up at the banker. "What do you use this thing for?"

"Paper knife. It's a souvenir."

"From Count Kotrzina? I'll bet it's a hell of a souvenir. He has had some wonderful times with knives. What does this gift commemorate?"

"I say, when the devil are you talking about? I barely knew the count. You—"

"I know, I'm being cheeky again. So you barely knew him, did you?"

Hewitt stood up to hand the telegram across the desk to him. Makenroy retreated to read it by the light of a window, saw what it was, and angrily folded it and put it in his shirt pocket. He held up the cigar and glanced smilingly at Vi, to ask her permission. He turned back to Hewitt, and they merely looked at each other a moment before Makenroy turned sidewise to light the cigar.

"Hewitt, I'm going to insist that you leave my house. God knows I regret being forced to do this, in Mrs. Chaney's presence, but your behavior is abominable, even for a private detective. I hope you aren't going to create a scene, because I mean to see your back once and for all, even if it means calling in my men to evict you with force. Now, do be a good chap, and go decently."

He puffed away, turning the cigar to light it evenly. Hewitt took the knife by the tip, leaned back in his chair, raised his right hand above and behind his head, and let go.

He was by no means confident of his throw, but he did not much care. He knew he was good with a knife, but no man can trust a strange knife, and he had never cared much for throwing by the tip. He meant to give it exactly a turn and a half, and he estimated the distance at about twelve feet.

He was either lucky or better than he thought. The knife was completing its last spin when one of its keen edges slid through the top half of Makenroy's cigar. It thudded point first into a crude Indian-made statue of some saint or other, carved from ebony. It went in deeply enough to stick there, vibrating violently for a moment.

Makenroy turned his whole body stiffly, shuffling his feet around like an old, old man, with the half-severed cigar dangling from his mouth. "Jesus Christ, you could have cut my face off," he stammered. "You ruffian, that was a dashed risky thing to do."

Hewitt took his .45 out of his belt holster, pulled back the hammer, and pointed it at the banker's belly.

"Do you think I would care if I had cut your head off? Do you think it would bother me to blow your heart out right now? Do you think anybody in Matamoros would shed a tear for you? Why, they'd carry me through the town on their shoulders, if I shot you. Do you think anybody in the government of Mexico would do anything but rejoice? I've got more friends there than you have," he said.

"You son of a bitch, I came in here and gave you a chance to save the family honor that you had thrown away. I saved your miserable life, as well as your miserable money. You were so infatuated with your fellow nobleman that I had to talk to you like a halfwit. I should have walked out and let you handle it yourself.

"Do you wonder why I didn't? For the same reason that you have done every low, thieving, cheating, conniving thing you have done in your life in Mexico—money! I knew your written bond was no better than your word, and that I would have to collect the hard way when it came time. It never did worry me, collecting from someone like you.

"I want fifteen thousand dollars in cash, and I want those one hundred counterfeit coins, and if I don't get them, I'm going to kill you right here in this room. I'll collect a lot more than fifteen thousand from your accounts. I can go through your books and find enough loans to settle our bill before you're cold, Makenroy. All I have to do is offer your Mexican borrowers their notes back, and I'm a rich man. Make up your mind now, Makenroy—*now!*"

The banker's face had gone gray in color and wet with sweat. He stared a moment at Hewitt, eyes protruding glassily, and then looked around at Vi.

He burst out, "Great God, Mrs. Chaney, the bounder means to kill me! This is robbery at gunpoint."

Vi nodded cheerfully. "I'm afraid so, and I'm a one-third partner. Do you remember the night you were in Austin, just before Dad died, and you brought some wine and Swiss chocolates to the house?"

"Yes, but—"

"The papers were full of some scandal or other, about some titled Englishman and his own niece. And you told Dad, 'When an English nobleman goes bad, he falls so far that the dregs of every other nation look down on him.' Do you remember that?"

"I don't know. I may have said it. The man has a gun on me, do you realize that, Mrs. Chaney?"

She opened her big purse and took out her .38. "I carry one too." She put the gun back. "Do you want me to tell Mr. Hewitt why you had to leave England?"

"What!"

"You heard me! Shall I tell him why you have buried yourself here in Matamoros all these years?"

"Blackmail, blackmail," he said hoarsely. He turned to Hewitt. "I haven't fifteen thousand in the house."

"You better have."

"I can't give you what I haven't got. I'm only a bank of deposit. I can't give away my clients' funds. Even if I had them on hand. Have mercy, man! Give me a few days. Fifteen thousand—why, do you realize how little I make here? How long it would take me to save that much again?"

Hewitt said nothing, but the muzzle of the .45 followed every movement Makenroy made. Twenty minutes later, they walked out of the house with $15,000 in American currency, plus the two hundred counterfeit slicks. The *mozo* brought the rig to the gate. Hewitt helped Vi in, got in beside her, and handed the *mozo* a *peso.*

"Gracias, hombre. Que tenga buena suerte," he said.

The mozo saluted him with dignity. Hewitt chirped to the horses, which broke into a trot.

"Aren't you afraid he'll take a pot shot at you from a window?" Vi asked him.

"Nope."

"I am. Aren't you afraid he'll send ahead and have us detained at the border?"

"Nope."

"That's what I call nerve." She laid her hand on his arm. "But I know you better than he does. You never would have killed him in cold blood. Jeff, it was a wonderful bluff but that's all it was—a bluff."

He met her eyes. "What did he do, to get him run out of England?"

"I haven't the faintest idea."

"Well, then!"

She laughed joyously. "Oh Jeff, we're a pair to draw to, aren't we?" He did not answer, and in a moment she went on seriously, "All this has been exciting, and God knows I was bored to death. For me, being a widow-lady on a cattle ranch is slow death. Just before I heard from Johnny, saying if I'd come to Austin, he'd have some work for me, do you know what I was doing?"

"I wouldn't try to guess."

"I had a big garden this year, and I've got a cart that holds a hundred gallons of water, and a lazy old mule to pull it. I had some choice tomato plants that I raised in a cold frame and set out with my own hands. I took good care of all but one of them. That one was me, Jeff. I hardened my heart and walked right past it without stopping my mule, just to see how long it would live without water.

"Every living thing needs to be refreshed, each thing according to its own needs. My tomato plant needed water. The others grew and grew, and had set on bushels of big, beautiful tomatoes before I left. The one that was me just shriveled up, and got weaker and uglier and more hopeless."

"Until it died?"

"Not quite," she said with a laugh. "The day I got Johnny's letter, which refreshed me, I took pity on it and watered it, too. Oh, Jeff, let's do something this afternoon, something that isn't work! Do you like to hunt prairie chickens?"

He said, "Most of the time, yes. Anything I can eat, I like to hunt—most of the time. But when I have just finished a case, especially a brutal one like this one, I turn against any kind of violence for a while."

She snatched his hand up and kissed the back of it. "I'm glad you told me that. Can we just go for a ride, then? Just be together, be ourselves, have a picnic, maybe."

"Let's see if we can fix it up with Mrs. Frank to pack some lunch for us, and I'll get a bucket of ice, and put a few bottles of beer in it. Do you drink beer?"

"I'm a Texas lady, Jeff. You know the old Panhandle saying about sin, don't you?"

"I've never heard that one, I guess."

"That when the hot, dry winds blow, it's no sin to get drunk, and when the cold winter northers blow, it's no sin to commit adultery, and when absolutely nothing else is happening, it's no sin to pick a fight. They call that the Law of Deef Smith."

Their eyes met. "How about when it's hot and humid?" he asked.

"I guess you follow your conscience," she said, coloring deeply.

They drove out into the dunes northwest of town, found some shade, and put a horse blanket on the ground under a warty little tree that gave little or no shade. They ate ham sandwiches, drank beer, and swatted sand fleas until they had to give up. They returned to the buggy and started back, early in the afternoon.

"I won't mind going back to the ranch for a while, now," she said pensively.

"You should be able to buy yourself some more good property, now. From what I hear about Texas ladies, all they want is the land next to theirs," he said.

"We're really going to make some money, aren't we?"

"Probably not as much as we deserve. Look, here's how I figure it out. We're supposed to get ten thousand reward for catching the killer of the bank messenger, Chester Larrick, plus half of the money recovered from the theft, and Johnny is taking back sixty-one thousand, three hundred dollars," he said.

"You brought back Si Taylor's ten thousand, and we now have Lawrence Makenroy's fifteen thousand, so there's no way we're going to be cheated on that. The Treasury is supposed to come through with thirty thousand, and according to my partner, Kotrzina's family is offering a reward of a little more than four thousand, in gold marks, for information as to the whereabouts of their missing sprig of nobility."

"And we can sure as the dickens supply that," Vi murmured.

"Yes, only I don't trust nobility any farther than I do the Treasury Department. Look, here's how it works out so far."

He stopped the team, got a piece of paper and pencil from his pocket, and listed the same figures he was going to have to list for Conrad Meuse, when he got home to Cheyenne. There was always a dispute with Conrad, usually about expenses; and since Conrad was the accountant and financial wizard, he was a hard man to beat. This was good practice for Hewitt:

Reward for killer of Chester Larrick	$10,000.00
One half of $61,300, recovered for Great Coast Bank and Trust Company	30,650.00
30% of $10,000 recovered for Si Taylor	3,000.00
Reward from Lawrence Makenroy	15,000.00
Reward from U. S. Treasury Department	30,000.00
Reward from Kotrzina family	4,000.00
TOTAL TO BE SHARED	$92,650.00
Each partner's share	$30,883.33

"That leaves us all butting heads for an odd penny, but let's don't start practicing yet," he said. "Scale the Treasury reward down to about ten thousand, and the Kotrzina

family reward down to about fifteen cents, and we'll probably come out a lot closer to about twenty-two or twenty-
three thousand dollars each. And if Great Coast Bank and
Trust gets tough, and Johnny forgets to hide the bundle
until he has closed his deal, it could be less than that."

She drew a long breath. "It's more than I ever dreamed
of earning."

"My dear, the count could have made a lot of bad trouble
for the United States of America. I don't know enough
about international finance to speak with authority, but
Denny was scared, and the Secretary was scared. Panic is a
strange thing, whether it's in a crowded street or a broker-
age exchange, and no country is any better than its money.
That's why I don't mind being gouged a little by the Treasury. It's our country too."

She laid her cheek against his arm, and held it there.
"It's all right with me, too. What will you do now?"

"Change all the cash we have on hand into bank paper.
Give you your share, send Johnny's to his office, and send
mine to my partner."

"Then what?"

"I'm tired of Gulf Coast heat and humidity. This is a
good time of year to be in the Tetons, and I think I'm entitled to a vacation."

"Oh, me too!" she said with a tired sigh.

"Ever think of a summer in the Tetons?"

"I absolutely *never* think of mountains with such a lewd
name. You know what it means, of course."

"Yes, but I'm shocked that you do."

"I'm a Texas widow-lady, remember."

"I'm pretty footloose, my dear. Couple of days back in
Austin, and I'm ready to go. In case you decided to go too,
how long would you need?"

"Long enough to send the ranch a short telegram and buy a few clothes."

"I thought you just bought everything new."

"Just for Austin. When I ride a horse, I straddle it. When I camp, and sleep on the ground, and cook over a fire, I like Levi's, too."

She started to snuggle closer to him, but five tired cowboys who had been helping cut cattle for the shippers came up behind them on five tired horses. They were heading for their favorite Brownsville saloon or Matamoros *cantina,* and let nothing stand in their way! They tipped their hats to Vi and gave Hewitt the usual Texas greeting.

"Hidy, seh. Hidy. Hidy. Hidy, seh. Hidy."

"Gentlemen," he responded, touching his hat.

They rode out of sight, and he transferred the lines to one hand, to put the other arm around Vi. She reached up to give him a quick kiss on the cheek.

"But not to get married, Jeff," she said. "I wouldn't do that to you."

"Honey, never decide a problem before you have to. Why worry now about that or anything else? We've won a big one! Let the future take care of itself."

"All right. But my dear, I know myself, and I'm sure I know how I'll feel about that tomorrow, or two weeks from tomorrow, or two years. I think I love you very, very much, Jeff, but not enough to keep house for you forever," she said. "Maybe there'll come a time, someday, when men and women can work these things out. But now? And us? You know it wouldn't work. You *know* that!"

He did know it, and he felt a deep pang of sadness that matched that in her voice. One of the reasons they were both so good at this business was the lonely streak both had, which made them observers rather than participants in so many things in life. It was a heavy curse, yet even as

he decided that it was a curse, he was looking ahead beyond the Grand Tetons to the next job, the next case, the
next test of wits and talents. Which reminds me, he thought,
I've got to get a long telegram off to Conrad tonight. . . .